DAN DE LUCA

Copyright © 2024 Dan De Luca

All rights reserved.

ISBN: 9798339385523

DEDICATION

To Laura, Giuseppe, and Massimo – Your belief in me has been the key to everything I've achieved. Siete il mio cuore.

To the rest of my family – I am forever grateful for your unwavering support.

To Ken, my friend, creative partner, and cellmate in the entertainment industry – It's been one hell of a ride and I'm looking forward to more!

CONTENTS

1	MARY, MARY, QUITE CONTRARY	3
2	ALL IS NOT WELL	15
3	POSSESSION	28
4	INTERROGATION	32
5	BLOOD IN THE BUSINESS PARK	42
6	RITUALS OF DEATH	51
7	CONFESSION	60
8	MARCHING ORDERS	72
9	REFLECTIONS OF THE QUEEN	75
10	STALKED BY SHADOWS	88
11	THE HUNT	11
12	THE LAIR	110
13	WHISPERS IN THE DARK	120
14	INTO THE ABYSS	131
15	THE BAIT	144
16	VENGEANCE UNLEASHED	160
17	JUST OKAY	177
18	ASHES AND ECHOES	184

CHAPTER 1

MARY, MARY QUITE CONTRARY

Dim streetlights cast twisted shadows on the cracked pavement as three teenage boys slipped from one alley to the next. The air was thick with the stench of rotting garbage, but there was something else that made their skin crawl and their hearts pound - a primal fear that sent shivers down their spines. Despite the overwhelming insecurity, they moved with a sense of urgency and determination, fueled by a potent mix of anxiety and exhilaration coursing through their veins.

Leading the group was Trent Marakakis, standing over the others by at least four inches. On any other day, he might have been considered ruggedly handsome, but today his face was pale and slick with a constant sheen of sweat. His brown hair was matted with dirt and perspiration clinging to his forehead. Yet, underneath the unkempt appearance, there was an undeniable allure - a dangerous charm that drew the others to follow in his footsteps. There was a roughness to him that spoke of experiences far beyond his years. Trent held onto a small can of gasoline as if it were a prized possession - both to be feared and revered.

Close behind Trent was Jordy Shulle, a lanky teenager with greasy black hair. His face was pockmarked and constantly red from picking at it. He ran through the alley swinging a rusty pipe he found among the trash, and every time he swung it, he pretended he was fighting off a horde of rabid zombies. His pale blue eyes darted around, taking in their surroundings with a mix of excitement and curiosity. This is what he lived for - the danger and the thrill of being part of something bigger than himself.

Bobby Smalls lagged behind, pushing up his thick-rimmed glasses as he caught his breath. The extra weight around his waist made it difficult for him to keep up and caused him to sweat profusely on the unusually warm evening. He wasn't one for trouble, but the need to belong pushed him forward despite the doubts nagging at the back of his mind. His steps faltered and his feet dragged as if weighed down by the heavy atmosphere. His heart raced with warning signals that he knew he should listen to. But he took a deep breath and forced himself forward, pushing his sweat-soaked dirty blond hair out of his face with each step - silently arguing against turning back.

As they ventured deeper into the unknown, the narrow alleys seemed to blend one into the other. They didn't know how far they'd gone, or even how to get back to where they started. It was a confusing maze of alleyways haphazardly situated behind the city's now long-forgotten neighborhood of row houses. They felt invincible at that moment - fueled by youthful recklessness and a false sense of confidence.

When they passed the last streetlamp, its light started to disappear slowly into the surrounding blackness as if it were being sucked away into the night. Smalls' hands trembled as he clutched at his shirt, twisting the fabric between his fingers. He tried to steady himself and push down the panic, but it was useless. It clawed its way up, threatening to choke him.

"Come on, Smalls," Jordy taunted, his voice cutting through the silence like a knife. "You wanted to tag along."

"Maybe we should just head back and try again tomorrow," Smalls suggested, his voice trembling with the hope that the others might listen, that they might turn back before they went any further.

As soon as Smalls uttered those words, Trent blazed with anger as he abruptly turned to face Smalls, clenching his jaw so tightly that his muscles twitched. Smalls instinctively stepped back, feeling his pulse quicken as Trent pulled up his left sleeve, revealing a gruesome stump where his hand used to be.

Trent pointed an accusing finger at Smalls. His face twisted into a contorted mask of pure hatred as he growled, "She's the reason for all of this! That old Hag placed a curse on me, and she's gonna pay for it."

Smalls froze, the reality of Trent's words sinking in like a cold wave. The tales and whispers about the "Hag" were familiar to everyone, but Smalls had never taken them seriously. It was just a myth, a story concocted to frighten children. But now, looking at Trent's mutilated hand, Smalls couldn't deny the possibility that there might be some truth behind the tales. The damage done to Trent's hand was too severe to ignore; it looked as if it had melted away like a candle under its flame.

Jordy swung his pipe and laughed, a harsh, mocking sound that grated on Smalls' nerves. "We'll make her regret it tonight," he said with a smirk, a confidence in his voice that Smalls found unsettling.

At the turn of the next alley, Smalls hesitated. His feet planted to the ground as if he were contemplating turning back. He swallowed hard and glanced at Trent and Jordy, then at the long dark alley ahead. The feeling persisted that they were about to enter something far more risky than they realized. But Trent's anger and Jordy's bravado pushed them forward. Smalls had always been the follower, tagging along behind stronger, more confident boys, hoping for a scrap of their respect or even just an ounce of their approval. But true respect was something he had never earned from them or anyone else. He was constantly the target of their jokes, pushed around like a punching bag, always on the outside looking in.

They marched in silence until suddenly Jordy recoiled in disgust. "Oh, fuckin' a," he muttered, realizing there was dog shit smeared on the pipe he was carrying. Without a second thought, he wiped it off on Smalls' jacket.

The gesture snapped something in Smalls. He'd had enough—enough of the apprehension, enough of Jordy's taunts, enough of being trodden upon. He shoved Jordy hard, his irritation boiling over.

"What the hell, man?" Jordy stumbled back, surprise flashing across his face.

"You think this is funny?" Smalls snapped, his frustration fueled a newfound strength within him. "Look at what you did to my jacket!" His hostility may have been aimed at Jordy, but it was directed at something deeper. He dreaded facing his father and the inevitable lecture that would follow his trying to explain what happened to his brand-new jacket.

Jordy's expression shifted from shock to amusement, a chuckle bubbling up as he tried to brush it off. "Relax, Smalls. It was just a joke."

Smalls ripped off his jacket and hurled it at Jordy with a vicious force that narrowly missed his head. "You asshole!" The words spat out of him like a punch as his face contorted with indignation.

Jordy instinctively raised the pipe in defense, but Trent stepped between them, his fist clenched tightly and ready for a fight. "That's enough!" he barked, his voice booming with authority. His intense gaze locked onto Jordy with an unrelenting determination, sending a chill down his spine and silencing any retort he might have had.

Jordy's grit wavered, his bravado crumbling under Trent's glare. He stumbled back lowering the pipe, his shoulders slumping as he glanced away, suddenly finding the cracked pavement more interesting than the confrontation. "Yeah… yeah, okay," he muttered, glancing cautiously at Smalls before turning to walk away.

Smalls watched him distance himself, a mix of relief and disappointment churning in his gut. He had always wanted to confront Jordy, but that moment had passed along with his fleeting feeling of courage. As they continued forward in silence, the night air felt thick and heavy, whispering secrets he didn't want to hear.

As they rounded the corner, the light from the last streetlight faded completely behind them, leaving the alleyway cloaked in moonlight. The dimness played tricks on them, distorting the figure hunched over in front of them. Her face was obscured by grime and tangled hair, making her blend into the garbage strewn around her. As they drew nearer, they saw the deep wrinkles etched into her skin and the signs of decay that clung to her like a frightening memory. She wore tattered gray clothing that hung loosely on her frail frame, and her eyes were dull and sunken, like those of a stuffed deer head in an abandoned hunting lodge.

The woman smelled of stale sweat and the musty scent of unwashed clothes. The smell was stifling, like a damp basement layered with the scent of something rotting beneath it all. If they had ever smelled the smell of death, this was it, or something close to it.

Trent motioned for Jordy to flank her as they approached. He nodded and disappeared around the corner and out of sight. "Hey, you old hag!" Trent shouted, his voice laced with anger and hatred. The woman froze, her gaze darting between the boys with a mix of suspicion and defiance.

Blinded by hate, Trent moved closer to the woman, the gasoline can swinging at his side. "You did this to me, didn't you?" He accused, his voice trembling with emotion as he revealed his stump of a hand. "Now you're gonna burn like the witch you are."

The old woman's gaze was cold and calculating. The boys shifted uneasily, glancing at each other, their bravado fading. Smalls' grip tightened on his shirt, but he didn't move, his feet rooted to the spot as Trent's words remained unanswered. Smalls turned to Trent cautiously, his voice barely above a whisper. "Hey, man, maybe we should just go," he suggested, his nerves fraying at the edges.

Trent's hatred had consumed him; he was no longer rational. "I told you no!" he bellowed, not even looking at Smalls. His expression was wild and his fists clenched tightly around the gasoline can. The old woman dropped her bag and stood still, poised for action with a makeshift machete sneaking out from her sleeve. It glistened under the faint moonlight that trickled into the alley.

She appeared unfazed by the threats being thrown her way, showing no reaction, flinching, or blinking. It was as if Trent were speaking in a language she couldn't comprehend. Instead, she began to sing softly and slowly, "Mary, Mary, quite contrary..." Smalls shuffled away nervously as Trent unscrewed the cap on the gasoline can and waved it at her, threateningly shaking it in front of her face. But the old woman remained in place, gripping the machete firmly and ready to strike if necessary.

Trent's eyes gleamed with madness as he lunged forward, splashing gasoline from the rusty can onto the woman. The stench filled the narrow alley, foreboding and ominous. She raised her machete up high. But before she could strike - CRACK! The sound of metal against bone echoed off the graffiti-streaked walls, followed by the sickening thud of her body collapsing on the hard pavement. The machete fell from her limp grip and clattered to the ground.

Jordy stepped back from behind, still clutching the shit-stained pipe that glinted with a grim satisfaction. A cruel grin spread across his face, sending chills down Smalls' spine as he stumbled away in fear.

"Yeah, bitches! Home run!" Jordy exclaimed, his voice full of satisfaction as he mimicked swinging a bat and hitting a home run with his pipe.

The three boys stood in silence, their adrenaline pumping as they stared down at the unconscious woman. Jordy smiled with perverse gratification, but Smalls looked uneasy. "What did you do?" Smalls asked, his voice trembling.

Jordy just laughed and kicked the old woman hard in the back. "She deserved it," Trent said with a sneer.

Smalls shook his head in disbelief. "That's enough, we should go!" He begged, turning to leave.

Trent grabbed Smalls by the arm. "You ain't going anywhere you little shit. We're in the together," he said, pulling him back towards the woman's body. At that moment Smalls regretted having ever agreed to follow them. Only now he realized it would have been better to be mocked than be in this godforsaken alley with Trent, Jordy, and some homeless woman whose only crime was minding her own business.

Jordy's cruel laughter echoed through the abandoned alleyway as he lunged toward the defenseless woman with a vicious kick. The sound of bones cracking and snapping filled the air as his boot connected with her body, but she showed no sign of pain. In a flash, the Hag's hand shot out like a striking cobra, snatching his foot in a vice-like grip. The three boys gasped in disbelief as she leapt to her feet crushing Jordy's foot like a tin can, her face contorted in fury and determination.

Her body, marked by heavy scars beneath her tattered clothes, bore the evidence of battles fought and won. With cold fury and unyielding strength, she held Jordy off balance, gripping his leg in midair, her hand relentlessly crushing bone as he squealed in pain.

"No!" Smalls cried out in distress, taking a few hesitant steps backward, practically tripping over himself.

The Hag's face twisted in unbridled fury as she ripped the pipe from Jordy's trembling hand. With a primal scream, she rammed it into his mouth, his shrieks cut short as his teeth shattered under the force. The impact was so brutal it lifted him off the ground, pinning him to the unforgiving alley wall. Blood erupted in a violent spray, splattering the scene in a sickening shade of crimson.

Trent watched in horror as the woman he had underestimated revealed herself to be a fierce force to be reckoned with, unstoppable in her tenacity for vengeance. The once-desolate alleyway now felt claustrophobic and menacing, filled with the raw power emanating from the Hag as she sought retribution.

She let out a savage cry as she picked up her machete and swung it toward Trent's head. Like a well-trained boxer, he managed to dodge the blade at the very last second. Smalls watched in horror as Trent splashed gasoline all over her, the noxious fumes billowing out, making them both cough and wheeze.

He slammed his lighter open, its menacing flame cast harsh streaks across his face as he taunted the old woman with it, forcing her to shrink back. Smalls looked at him with bewilderment, realizing he fully intended to burn the homeless woman alive.

The Hag stepped towards Trent and swung her machete, snuffing out the flame. He fumbled to relight his lighter. CLICK. CLICK. CLICK. His nerves were electric and about to explode. Finally, a blue flame emerged and quickly turned yellow.

With a swift flick of his wrist, he tossed the lighter onto the Hag's body, and she erupted into flames with startling speed and ferocity. With a bloodcurdling scream, she swung her machete wildly in every direction, her movements becoming more erratic as the fire consumed her. Searing heat radiated from the burning figure forcing the two boys to step back.

The smell of burning flesh filled the air, causing the boys to gag. The Hag's screams turned into gurgles as she coughed up blood and bile. She writhed in agony until she convulsed one last time and fell to the ground in a smoldering heap.

Trent recoiled in horror, unable to look away from the woman engulfed in flames. His initial fury was quickly replaced with overwhelming dread. A wave of guilt washed over him, as he realized he had just taken someone's life.

Trembling, Smalls sprinted down the desolate alleyway trying to find his bearings and that last streetlight they passed. His tears blurred his vision as he struggled to process the traumatic scene that played out before him: Jordy's brutal death, and the burning of the Hag. Panic surged through his veins, fueling his desperate escape.

But as he ran, a sinking feeling settled in his stomach. The maze of twisting alleyways disoriented him, and he realized with growing apprehension that he was hopelessly lost. The atmosphere seemed to smother him, trapping him in its claustrophobic embrace. His legs burned with exhaustion, each step heavier than the last. Sweat dripped down his face, mingling with his tears and stinging his eyes. He finally collapsed against a brick wall, gasping for air and trying to push away the overwhelming dread that threatened to consume him. So many questions raced through his mind - would Trent come after him? Would anyone believe what happened here?

A rustling noise behind him jerked Smalls out of his thoughts. Shuddering, he turned to see Trent emerging from the shadows of the alleyway. Anxiety pulsed through every nerve in Smalls' body as he took a step back. But as Trent came closer, Smalls noticed something different about him - he looked smaller and weaker, his face twisted with shock and guilt. A wave of conflicting emotions washed over Smalls - a mixture of panic and exasperation mingled with confusion and a touch of sympathy for Trent.

"What did you do?" Smalls asked, his voice shaky.

Trent didn't respond at first, his steps were slow and deliberate as he approached Smalls. He backed away until he hit the cold, unforgiving brick wall behind him.

"Why did you do that?" Smalls' voice trembled as he repeated his question, his agitation bubbling over into anger. Tears ran down Trent's face as he finally spoke, his voice breaking.

"She killed Jordy," Trent choked out, the words heavy with sorrow.

"He tried to kill her!" Smalls shouted. "Why couldn't you just stay away from her? Now we're murderers! Why didn't you just listen..." He stopped himself, knowing it was pointless to continue. The two boys stood face to face, trapped in a tangled mess of repercussions they never could have predicted. Each one trying to come to terms with the gravity of their actions.

They looked at each other searching for answers but finding only emptiness and despair. Trent's body trembled violently before finally succumbing to the weight of his guilt, collapsing to his knees with a ragged cry. He raised his mangled hand, barely recognizable as flesh, and wept uncontrollably. "I didn't mean to do this," he wailed, choking on each syllable. "I just... I didn't know what to do." The plea in his voice was raw and broken, begging for forgiveness and mercy.

Smalls couldn't believe what had happened. His resentment towards Trent burned hot, but his heart also ached with empathy for the only person he could turn to. As he slowly approached Trent, his mind was torn between wanting to distance himself and offering comfort.

He placed a shaky hand on Trent's shoulder, trying to push away the anxiety that threatened to consume him. In the alley's decay, surrounded by crumbling buildings and fading city lights, the boys clung to each other as their last source of hope.

But deep down, Smalls couldn't shake off the turmoil inside him - torn between betrayal and loyalty for his troubled friend.

CHAPTER 2

ALL IS NOT WELL

Ken Walsh lay sprawled on the worn leather couch in Luca's sparse apartment, the kind of place that whispers of functionality over comfort. It was three in the morning, and the green neon light from the liquor store across the street seeped through the blinds, washing the room in an eerie, ghostly hue. He wore a t-shirt and boxers as he slept, while the rest of his clothes were abandoned on the floor, evidence of a late-night scotch-induced haze.

Ken's phone buzzed on the coffee table, casting a bright blue light across his weary face. He let out a grumble before attempting to move, his body feeling heavy and uncooperative. With a strained effort, he managed to sit up, his aging joints protesting with every movement. He ran a hand through his messy hair, or what was left of it, as he squinted at the glaring screen in front of him and reluctantly answered. The voice on the other end was abrupt and jarring compared to the quiet stillness around him.

"Walsh?" the voice barked.

Ken blinked, trying to shake off the fog of sleep. "What is it? It's three in the damn morning!" he snapped back, irritation clear in his tone. He listened as patiently as he could, his face gradually hardening as the details of a new crime scene were relayed to him. There was a moment of silence before he sighed, resigned. "Okay, I'm there," he muttered, ending the call.

Ken sat for a moment, taking deep breaths and trying to shake off the grogginess from his sleep. He had been staying at Luca's place for about two weeks now, but being woken up in an unfamiliar apartment still threw him off. It took him a few seconds to remember where he was.

He swung his legs down from the couch and reached for his clothes. He hastily put on a wrinkled button-down shirt and rumpled chinos that were clearly past their prime. A sports jacket hung on a nearby chair, and he grabbed it along with his service revolver and shoulder holster before making his way down the hallway. His unkempt appearance only added to the sense of urgency he felt. It was the desperate routine of a man living a life filled with midnight calls and hurried exits.

Ken stopped outside Luca's bedroom door and gently knocked. "Marchetti?" he said softly not wanting to disturb anyone else who may be inside. After a moment, he heard some rustling before Luca appeared in the doorway, wearing a polo shirt and loose slacks haphazardly hanging on his hips. Despite the sleepiness in his hazel eyes, they sharpened when they saw Ken. "What's going on?" Luca asked, looking up at Ken, who towered over him by four inches."Dispatch needs us on location," Ken replied, his voice heavy with the weight of yet another unscheduled interruption. Luca nodded, not needing more details. This was their life, their routine, and it was the one they'd grown accustomed to over the years.

Ken's gaze drifted to the bed behind Luca, where a woman lay sprawled beneath a sheet that barely covered her lower back. He could feel Luca's watching him as he quickly looked away, feeling his face flush with embarrassment. "I didn't... I didn't mean to," Ken stammered, rubbing the back of his neck in discomfort. He tried to avoid Luca's knowing smile.

Luca smirked and closed the bedroom door behind him. "Get enough of a look?" he teased, his tone both playful and reprimanding.

"No, I swear, I didn't mean to," Ken muttered, clearly flustered. He followed Luca into the kitchen, trying to shake off the awkwardness of the moment.

The kitchen stood in stark contrast to the rest of the spotless apartment, boasting shiny stainless steel appliances and neatly arranged cookbooks. Ken couldn't help but notice a worn Bible placed next to a stack of Italian recipe books, an intriguing combination that piqued his interest. He arched an eyebrow but didn't say anything, simply observing as Luca effortlessly moved around the kitchen, brewing a fresh pot of Italian mocha coffee. Ken knew about Luca's past as a priest, then a husband, then a divorcee who ended up here. Despite their close friendship, they both avoided delving into each other's personal histories, respecting each other's privacy and understanding that if there was something important to share, the other would reveal it in their own time.

"Dispatch said there's a double homicide on the East End," Ken explained, his voice flat as Luca filled the pot with water and scooped in the near-black espresso grounds.

"It'd be nice if people stopped killing each other in the middle of the night," Luca retorted, his tone dry, but there was a whiff of amusement in his tone. Ken smiled, a rare expression on his usually stoic face.

"Can't pick the time for a murder, can you?" Ken responded, as Luca lit the stove, and within a few minutes the aroma of brewing coffee began to spread throughout the small kitchen.

"Who called it in?" Luca asked.

"Anonymous," Ken replied never moving his gaze from the mocha coffee maker that intrigued him so much.

Luca poured them each a small cup of espresso, the hot liquid steaming as it hit the cool air. Ken took a sip, savoring the bitter warmth that jolted his senses awake. It was one of the few things he enjoyed about being kicked out of the house he had known for fifteen years—the coffee was strong and rich, a far cry from the weak brew he was used to.

"We better head out soon," Ken said, setting his cup down with a firm clink against the countertop with a clink. "I want to get there before the sun rises and the lookie-loos crowd the scene."

Luca nodded, running his fingers through his thick salt and pepper hair to try and tame it. He was already shifting into work mode, his mind turning. "Do we have any info on the victims?" he asked, his voice calm, detached—a necessity in their line of work.

Ken frowned, trying to recall the brief details from the phone call. "Young man, homeless woman. No apparent motive yet," he replied, the furrow in his brow deepening as he thought.

Luca nodded and drained the last of his espresso before grabbing his coat. Without another word, the two men headed out of the apartment, the door clicking shut behind them with a finality that signals the start of another long day.

***

The streets were eerily quiet at this hour, the city seemingly asleep, but Ken and Luca knew better, this city never really slept.

The drive to the crime scene was quiet, the only sound was the low hum of the engine and the occasional wail of a distant siren. Ken gripped the wheel loosely, his fingers drummed a tune in his head. Luca stared out the window watching nothing in particular, his mind elsewhere.

Ken broke the silence, his voice tinged with curiosity. "So, who's the dame?" he asked, glancing over at Luca.

Luca didn't answer right away, still lost in his thoughts. After a moment, he shrugged, a hint of a smile playing at the corners of his mouth. "Tanisha… no, Tamika… I'm not sure," he admitted a hint of embarrassment in his voice.

"Sounds serious," Ken joked with a smile, but the levity was short-lived. His tone shifted, growing more serious. "She sent me the papers."

Luca turned to look at him, his expression softening. "She, as in your wife?" he asked, his voice gentle, almost cautious.

Ken grunted in response, bitterness laced his words. "Soon to be ex," he corrected, the weight of the situation pressing down on him.

Luca nodded, showing his sympathy. "Welcome to the club, my friend," he said quietly making it evident it wasn't a club he wanted to be a part of. The two men lapsed back into silence, each lost in their own thoughts as they approached the crime scene.

The alley was a hive of activity, lit by the harsh glare of police floodlights. In the early morning light, Ken and Luca made their way through the bustling scene, their faces serious and resolute. The air was thick and moist, evidence of the warm summer night that had just passed.

As they approached, they noticed the uniformed officer standing guard. Without a word, they flashed their badges and the officer stepped aside, allowing them to enter the crime scene.

Ken and Luca took in the flurry of activity around them, the officers and CSI techs moving with purpose as they gathered evidence and took measurements. The detectives could see the dedication and determination in their faces, knowing that they were all working towards one common goal.

Detective Mason acknowledged their approach with a tired yet professional expression. He was a tall, slender man with a bald head and rich mocha-colored skin, emanating an air of authority that demanded respect. "We have two victims," he gestured to the alley behind him. "Seventeen-year-old Jordy Shulle was reported missing last night. And we have a Jane Doe, homeless with no fixed address." As he spoke, his phone buzzed, and he glanced at the caller ID before excusing himself to take the call. As he stepped away, the disturbing scene behind him came into full view. Jordy Shulle's body hung against the wall, a pipe jammed into his mouth, his gaze frozen in a wide-eyed stare that mocked life. His body hung unnaturally still as if opposing gravity by hovering just inches above the ground. Six hours had passed since his death, making his skin pale and waxy, with blotches where blood had collected in his hands. Rigor mortis had set in, locking his limbs in place with a stiff and rigid hold, his hands curled into claw-like shapes. The face was expressionless, staring vacantly into nothingness. A faint odor of decay began to linger, and a slight bloating in the abdomen hinted at the onset of decomposition. The clothes, now ill-fitting, clung awkwardly to the stiffened body, giving it an eerie, almost unnatural appearance. The figure seemed to be suspended between life and death, serving as a poignant reminder of the ever-present march of time.

"How the hell did..." Ken couldn't finish his sentence bewildered by the physics of someone having jammed a pipe through the kids mouth and pinned him to the wall.

Ken and Luca exchanged a knowing look, a silent acknowledgment of the gravity of this case. It was unlike any other homicide they'd worked on before - more violent, more inhumane. As they approached the scene, a feeling of unease washed over them; something just felt off. They couldn't quite pinpoint what it was, because it was unlike anything they had ever encountered.

For the first time in his career, Ken was stunned as he took in the grotesque tableau, a chill crept up his spine. Luca scanned the scene with a frown as if he were trying to decipher a mystery that refused to come into focus. The coroner, Jenna Grimes, was crouched near the second body ready to cover it with a sheet. Jenna's face was stoic, a mask of professional detachment. But there was a stiffness in her posture, a subtle concern that betrayed her discomfort. Ken approached her, his focus fixed on the burnt remains of the homeless woman lying at her feet.

"Can we get a closer look?" Ken asked, his voice a mix of curiosity and apprehension.

Grimes nodded and handed them a pair of gloves. "Please be cautious," she warned, her gaze fixed towards Luca, who was known for spotting things others may have missed. Grimes was passionate about her work, but in another life, she had different aspirations. Though tall and attractive, she could have pursued a career as a model, but her dream was to become a physician and save lives rather than examine the causes of death. Unfortunately, her grades were barely passing and the only residency program that accepted her led her down the path of becoming a pathologist. She took to it like a duck to water and before she could think twice she had proven herself as the best Coroner in the tristate area. Still for Jenna Grimes, the best at a job she never wanted was little consolation.

Ken and Luca slipped on the gloves and crouched down beside the body. The stench of burnt flesh and blood was overpowering, along with the acrid scent of death. Luca focused as he examined the charred remains, sifting through ash and debris until his fingers brushed against something metallic.

"Hold her up," Luca instructed his voice tight with concentration. Ken lifted the torso slightly, bits of the body's ash covering his hands. Luca tried to carefully maneuver the object free. What he thought might be a small jagged piece of metal trash was indeed something else. It was just the tip of the Hag's weapon. As the two men lifted the burnt corpse they revealed the homemade machete, jagged and cruel, designed for one purpose: to inflict maximum pain. But it wasn't a haphazardly fashioned piece of protection. This blade showed it was something more. There was a precision to it. Someone had taken the time to craft a blade by hand without using a forge or casting. This was made from discarded aluminum.

Most likely from the side of a house or discarded construction materials. It was hammered, folded, reinforced, serrated, sharpened, and had a handle made of leather strapping that was worn with years of use. It was a horrific piece of art—beautiful and deadly all at once.

"Jesus," Ken muttered, his face contorted in disgust. "That's not a weapon, that's a torture device."

Before Luca could respond, Mason called out to them from across the alley. "You're gonna wanna see this," he shouted, holding up a small school ID card. "Found it down one of the alleys in a jacket a couple of hundred yards away."

Ken and Luca exchanged a glance, then stood, nodding their thanks to Grimes as they headed toward Mason. The writing on the school ID card was clear. Under the picture of a chubby teenager read the name, Robert Smalls.

Grimes knelt down and reached for the sheet to cover the corpse, but her hand froze mid-motion. Something had caught her eye. *Did the charred remains of the old woman just move?* she thought, her gaze fixed on the lifeless form. She stared at the face—an unsettling blend of ash and bone, with teeth jutting out in a perpetual grimace.

Then, without warning, it blinked.

Grimes stood paralyzed, her mouth agape, horror flooding her senses. *It was alive, but how?* Before she could react, the Hag's blackened hand shot up, seizing Grimes' wrist with a serpent-like speed and an unholy strength that threatened to snap her bones. Grimes was trapped, her body seized by an invisible force, trembling uncontrollably, unable to scream or pull away.

As Ken took the ID from Mason, a strange thud that caught Luca's attention. He turned to see Grimes now standing with her back to them, her face mere inches from the alley wall. Her body quivered, and she began muttering to herself, her words barely audible.

"Mary, Mary, quite contrary…" the words slipped from her lips, growing louder with each repetition. Luca froze in alarm as he realized something was terribly wrong.

She slammed her head against the brick wall with a sickening thud. "Ken!" Luca shouted, as he rushed toward Grimes.

Ken and Mason sprang into action, rushing over to assist. Despite their combined strength, the three of them struggled to pry Grimes away from the wall. Her body convulsed violently, as if she was in the midst of a seizure, her head repeatedly slamming against the brick wall. Suddenly, she turned and flung Mason across the alley as if he weighed nothing at all. He crashed to the ground, his breath knocked out of him as he clutched his chest in agony. "Holy shit," he wheezed, trying to regain his

"Jenna, stop!" Luca pleaded, but Grimes was beyond reason, slamming her head against the wall again and again with a stomach-churning sound. Blood poured down her face, and her skull cracked under the relentless assault.

"Habebō vindictam meam!" Grimes screamed, and the words were foreign and unnatural as they spilled from her mouth. With one final shuddering exhale, she collapsed into Luca's arms, her body limp and her face covered in blood.

Ken checked for a pulse, his hands shaking. "No pulse!" he yelled, panic creeping into his voice. Luca quickly laid her flat on the hard ground and instinctively began CPR compressions. Mason scrambled to retrieve a defibrillator from his vehicle.

As they struggled to rescue Grimes, a chilly breeze swept through the alley, even though the day ahead promised more sweltering heat. The tone shifted, growing eerie, more stifling, as if the alley itself was alive, watching and waiting.

He felt the wind roar around them before abruptly stopping, leaving behind an unsettling quiet. Luca's mind spun wildly as his face drained of color. "This can't be happening," he thought as he watched Grimes' body laying motionless between them, staring into the void while he kept up the compressions.

"She's gone," Ken sighed, his voice hoarse with disbelief.

Luca's breathing became panicked as he frantically pressed his hands against Grimes' chest, feeling the weight of her lifeless body beneath him. He paused, his fingers trembling as he searched desperately for a pulse on her cold neck, praying to God for any sign of life. "Come on, come on," he urged, his voice hoarse with desperation. Mason dashed down the alleyway returning with a bright blue and white briefcase. His expression was grim, but he was running on pure adrenaline. He knelt down hard on the pavement next to Grimes, scraping his knee and tearing a hole in his slacks. Without skipping a beat, he flipped open the briefcase to reveal the defibrillator. He flipped the switch on the instrument and prayed as the machine's winding whirring noise pierced the commotion.

Mason watched and waited as the digital readout on the case read "CHARGING." He readied himself and hovered the paddles over Grimes right upper chest just below the collarbone, and the other on the left side of the chest just below the armpit.

Luca reached in placing his fingers on her neck one last time. "Just maybe," he thought.

The defibrillator beeped loudly and unmistakably. The LED read "CHARGED" signaling it was ready to go. "Clear!" Mason yelled as he moved to place the paddles on Grimes's chest.

"Stop!" Luca's voice shook with urgency as he lunged forward, grabbing Mason's wrist in a tight grip. "She's still alive, but barely. If you shock her now, she won't make it." Mason froze, his hands trembling as he held the deadly paddles inches away from her chest. The rapid thumping of his heart echoed in his ears, and sweat dripped down his forehead as he fought to control his adrenaline-fueled panic.

Grimes jolted awake, coughing violently as if her lungs were being scorched from the inside out. Her throat felt raw and constricted as she struggled to catch her breath. Slowly, she became aware of her surroundings, blood dripped from her forehead, and the anxious faces of Ken, Luca, and Mason hovered over her.

"What happened?" Grimes managed to rasp out, her voice strained and weak. The throbbing in her head intensified with each passing second.

The men exchanged uneasy glances, unsure of how to explain what had just occurred. "Do you have a history of epilepsy?" Luca asked tentatively, his voice laced with concern.

Grimes shook her head, wincing at the sharp pain that shot through her skull. "No... never," she replied, feeling a sense of distress wash over her.

Mason spoke up, his tone was soft yet grave. "You had some kind of seizure," he said apologetically.

Distress gripped Grimes as she tried to piece together what was happening. Why was she on the ground? And why did these three men look so terrified? Before she could process anything further, Luca and Ken helped her to her feet.

"We need to get her to a hospital," Luca demanded with urgency as he looked at Mason, who nodded in agreement.

"They're gonna need the Coroner's wagon so I'll take her to St. Mary's," he confirmed, his voice strained with urgency. With a swift nod, they helped Grimes into Mason's car, both trying to get past the terrifying events that had just unfolded.

As Grimes settled in the back seat, Ken couldn't shake off the deep sense of unease that had made it's home in his gut. His hands clenched on the door handle as he replayed the gruesome scene in his mind.

Mason settled into the driver's seat, eagerly grasping the key. With a quick turn, the engine came to life and rumbled loudly. Across the crime scene, Luca retrieved the machete that had been placed in an evidence bag. He handed it through the passenger side window to Mason, who set it on the seat next to him. "Can you drop that off after you leave the hospital?" Luca asked, gesturing towards the evidence.

"No problem," Mason replied with a nod and a wave as Ken and Luca watched him drive away from the scene.

Luca turned to Ken and pulled out the student ID card from his pocket, studying it intently. "We need to find this Robert Smalls," he stated solemnly as he handed the ID card to Ken who nodded in agreement.

As they turned to leave, that familiar gust of wind whipped through the alleyway, sending shivers down their spines. It was a chilling reminder that this was no ordinary series of events, and there was still more to uncover.

CHAPTER 3

POSSESSION

The tires on Mason's car droned a monotonous tune as they rolled along the smooth asphalt. The hospital was only a few minutes away, but every second felt like an eternity, warped and stretched out of proportion. Every now and then, Mason stole a glance at Grimes slumped in the backseat. He couldn't help but replay the scene in his head repeatedly, asking himself the same question each time. How was it possible that this seemingly delicate woman could throw him with such ease?

The thought was unsettling enough to make beads of sweat form on Mason's forehead, even with the car's air conditioning blasting on high. Grimes sat in the backseat, motionless and vacant. Her once sharp eyes were now dull and unfocused, staring blankly through the dirty window.

It was as if she were there but not really there, her mind drifting off somewhere beyond reach. She seemed like a hollow shell of the person she used to be. Mason's grip tightened on the steering wheel, his knuckles turning white from the strain. He felt like he should say something, but the words were stuck in his throat, a mass of uncertainty and trepidation making it hard to speak.

"Are you okay back there?" he finally managed to choke out, his voice breaking through the heavy silence.

Mason could see her unblinking stare in the rearview mirror - no trace of recognition or response. It was like looking into the eyes of a lifeless doll, all surface with no depth.

"It'll be okay," he said in a feeble attempt at reassurance as they neared their destination. "We're almost there."

But as if a fissure had opened up in the earth beneath them, Grimes began to mutter under her breath - a sing-song whisper that sent shivers down Mason's spine.

"Mary, Mary, quite contrary," she murmured, the words slipping out like a heinous secret carried on a deathbed. "...how does your garden grow?"

CRACK!

The sound shattered the thin veneer of calm Mason was clinging to. He jerked his head towards the passenger side window, now splintered with a deranged-looking spiderweb of cracks, a smear of blood marking where Grimes had just slammed her head. Mason looked immediately for a place to pull over swerving the car and barely managing to dodge a fire hydrant near the sidewalk. He saw a wide enough shoulder on the side of the road and immediately wrenched the wheel to the right, the tires screeching on the gravel.

The car came to an abrupt standstill and dirt billowed up around the tires. The world outside was eerily quiet. He had pulled off near a husk of a business park that stood like a mausoleum to forgotten times. Mason turned, fearfulness clawing at his insides, to see Grimes staring directly at him. The calmness in her expression was more terrifying than any scream as he could see she was devoid of emotion.

"Grimes... please," Mason's voice cracked, barely above a whisper as blood trickled down her forehead and pooled into her left eye. He searched for any sign of recognition in her lifeless gaze. "What is it... say something!" But Grimes wasn't herself anymore. She had become something ancient and twisted. The sing-song chant resumed, more insistent now, as her body convulsed, her limbs jerked wildly like a marionette in the hands of an evil puppeteer. "With silver bells and cockle shells..."

Grimes' face twisted, her skin pulling unbearably tight over her cheekbones and her once smooth skin had become a sickly, ashen hue that caught the sunlight filtering into the car like a corpse under a flickering bulb. Her hair, once neatly bound, whipped around her face as if caught in an unseen wind, obscuring her features in a swirling rat's nest.

Mason watched frozen in a cocktail of horror and disbelief, as Grimes grabbed the machete from the bag in the front passenger's seat, a move so quick he had no time to react. The machete gleamed wickedly in the faint light, a harbinger of the violence to come. "Jenna, no, please!" Mason screamed as he fumbled to open the door. With a shriek, she swung the blade forward in a deadly arc. Her movements were jerky, almost mechanical, as though she moved by instinct alone, lacking any rational thought.

Just as he managed to grasp the door handle, pain exploded in Mason's neck. He was too late, the machete bit deep into his neck. Blood sprayed across the backseat, and the hot liquid splattered the interior in a gruesome pattern. Mason's hands flew to his throat, desperate to stem the flow of blood pouring forth, but it was too late. He felt the life draining out of him, his strength ebbing away with every passing second.

The creature that was Grimes—if she was still Grimes—continued her assault, and hacked away with wild abandon. The sickening crunch of bone and the squelch of flesh being torn apart filled the small space of the car. Mason's world slipped into a tunnel of pain, the edges of his vision eclipsing as his consciousness slipped away.

As Mason took his last breath, he locked eyes with Grimes - or what was left of her. Her once human and intelligent gaze had transformed into the predatory stare of a wild animal, gleaming with malicious joy. Her lips twisted into a wicked smile, revealing decaying and jagged teeth. With a ravenous appetite, she reached out and grasped Mason's severed head in her bony fingers. She lifted it to her face and inhaled deeply, savoring the metallic scent of his blood. Then, with disturbing pleasure, she tore the skin from his face with her sharp teeth, relishing in the taste and texture. And as she feasted, she chanted in a voice that was not hers and spoke ancient words in what seemed to be a summoning ritual.

CHAPTER 4

THE INTERROGATION

The police precinct blended into the city's edge like it belonged there, a relic from another era, fading but still holding the line. For years it had faithfully just done its job, standing tall and worn, indifferent to the world passing by. The statues of the twin lions out front were weathered and chipped, watching another day in the life of a city that didn't know how to quit. People had come and gone—some wary, some just tired—and the precinct had been there, doing what it did, no fanfare, no drama, just the quiet grind of the everyday.

Inside, the precinct was a hive of activity, officers and civilians alike caught in the web of law enforcement's relentless machinery. The walls were plastered with the faces of the wanted and the missing, grim reminders of the city's seedy undercurrents. The place smelled of stale coffee, sweat, and desperation, a combination of barely contained chaos.

Ken navigated swiftly through the busy lobby, his focus fixed straight ahead. Despite the hustle and bustle around him, he held the cup of coffee in his hand steady and untouched. His shoes struck the ground with a decisive rhythm, as if in sync with his unwavering focus. Finally, he arrived at a door adorned with a piece of paper listing reservation times and names scribbled in ink. He knocked firmly before being greeted by Detective Laura Weston. At first glance, she appeared taller than most women, with piercing green eyes and an air of authority. Ken always felt like he was being summoned to the principal's office whenever she asked to meet with him. Her curly chestnut hair was pulled tightly into a ponytail, highlighting her no-nonsense attitude,.

Laura was the head of the Special Victims Unit—a tight-knit squad that took on the worst of the worst: sexual assault, domestic violence, child endangerment. Her team had been sharp, focused, and trained to dig through the ugliest crimes. But Laura wasn't just a detective. She'd been an anchor for the whole department. Every morning, she'd commanded the briefings, setting the tone, getting the force ready to face whatever came next.

But to her the most important part of her job were the people. The victims. She was a shield for the broken, the vulnerable. Tough when she'd had to be, but there had always been this quiet compassion underneath it all, even as the nightmares she'd witnessed started to carve lines into her.

For Laura, it hadn't just been about closing cases. It had been about giving back the dignity life had taken from them.

Ken had understood that, he'd witnessed it first hand. He'd seen the way she'd moved, how hard she'd pushed. He'd respected her—no questions, no doubts. She'd earned it. Every bit and if she asked for something, he would do it without question.

The fluorescent lights in the cramped room were beating down on Vito Matthews, accentuating the circles under his eyes and the unshaven stubble on his chin. He sat slovenly in the metal chair, his shoulders sagging as he struggled to keep his eyelids from drooping. His clothes were rumpled, his face greasy, and the handcuffs around his wrists a stark contrast to the room's otherwise sterile order. The air was stale, heavy with the scent of foreboding and sweat, making the atmosphere that much more claustrophobic.

Laura stepped out into the hallway, the door clicking shut behind her. She exhaled sharply, her jaw straining as she met Ken's gaze, the furrow in her brow deepening with each passing second. "You okay?" She asked reading the expression on his face.

"Rough morning," he sighed. "You probably heard, double homicide on the East End of town."

"Yeah, they told me of the anonymous tip that came in," She nodded. "How's your daughter?"

"It's still difficult for her," Ken said choking up with emotion."

Laura rests a comforting hand on his shoulder more as a friend than a colleague. "It gets better, I promise."

Ken nods and purses his lips in a hopeful smile.

"I know this isn't your thing, but I thought maybe you could help," Laura admitted, her voice low. "Getting someone not in Special Victims to handle this would… well it would allow for me to… to be unaware of anything that might transpire behind that door."

Ken raised an eyebrow. Whatever she was proposing sounded like it was on the wrong side of being legal. All at once he felt relieved it wasn't about him, and at the same time, curious to what this straight edged Police Detective was asking. "What do you have?" He asked with genuine interest.

She nodded towards the closed door behind her, her lips thinning into a stern line. "Vito Matthews. He's a kid diddler. We've tried everything to keep this scum off the streets, but nothing sticks. We even applied for a Civil Commitment order, but you know how slow that process is."

Ken nodded understandingly, aware of the weight behind her words. A Civil Commitment order would essentially force the suspect into treatment against his will if it became impossible to incarcerate him. "He doesn't deserve any mercy," she sighed, frustration evident in her voice. It was a constant battle, an endless cycle of crime and punishment, and sometimes it felt like they were fighting a losing battle against criminals like Vito Matthews.

Ken peered through the narrow window, his gaze landing on Matthews, who was picking at the dry skin on the palms of his hands. He was the kind of man you wouldn't notice in a crowd, which was probably the point. Middle-aged, with thinning hair combed over in a half-hearted attempt to hide the inevitable. His face was pale, the kind that never saw much sun, and his eyes—small, darting— always seemed to be searching for something or someone. He had a paunch, the result of too many years sitting behind a desk but most likely in front of a TV.

His clothes were nondescript: a cheap, wrinkled shirt poorly tucked into pale grey faded slacks cinched just above his belly button and his shoes were scuffed revealing that had long since given up trying to make an impression. There was something about his smile, too—forced, never quite genuine—that made your skin crawl. He was the kind of person who slipped through the cracks, unnoticed, until it was too late, but there was also a hint of defiance in the set of his jaw, a hint of the arrogance he refused to let go.

"Cameras?" Ken asked looking in the back corners of the room through the door window where he could see a closed circuit camera.

"This one's out of order," she said softly, motioning towards the door. "It's scheduled to be fixed this afternoon. That's why I chose it."

"Tell the uniform to take a lunch break," Ken said under his breath. Laura looked at him and nodded her reply. He then handed her his service revolver, and with a silent understanding between them, she placed it at the small of her back.

"I owe you one," she said as she gave him a nod and returned to the interrogation room.

Ken moved away from the door and waited down the hall until Laura emerged with the uniformed officer in tow. The sound of her heels clicked against the tile floor as they walked past Ken and turned the corner, disappearing into the busy precinct.

Alone now, Ken waited for a few more people to pass by before making his way back to the interrogation room. He took the piece of paper off the door and covered the small window that looked inside.

With a deep breath, he opened the door and entered. His heavy footsteps echoed in the confined space, each step purposeful and calculated. Matthews looked up at him, a smug smirk spreading across his face that was betrayed by beads of sweat on his upper lip. It was the kind of smirk that suggested he thought himself untouchable and in control. Sadly, for years he had been able to manipulate the system thanks to a network of lawyers, psychiatrists, and paid-off witnesses, allowing him to continue indulging in his twisted desires without consequences.

Matthews sneered at him, his contempt evident in his voice. "You're wasting your time," he said. "I already told the broad, I don't know anything. And where's my lawyer? I'm not saying a word without my lawyer present. I know my rights," he added mockingly. They all knew their rights, every person he interrogated who was guilty beyond a doubt, said the same thing. Yet none of them seemed concerned about the rights of their victims.

Ken stepped closer to Matthews, his presence imposing, determined, and steadfast. The mood in the room crackled with the potential for violence, the kind that's been held in check for too long. He flexed his knuckles, the sound of them cracking one by one was like gunfire in the stillness.

The smirk on Matthews' face faltered slightly. He swallowed, the sound was loud in the quiet room. "You don't scare me," he sputtered, his voice shaking despite the swagger. Matthews could feel the tension emanating off of Ken, the promise of pain in the sternness of his face, the set of his shoulders. It was the kind of danger that doesn't need words, the kind that speaks through bulging veins and sharp tones. A volcano simmering, ready to blow.

Ken remained silent, knowing that words were futile when dealing with men like Matthews. Instead, he let the silence envelop them both, a tense and suffocating weight. As the seconds ticked by, Ken could see Matthews' cocky smirk fading, replaced by an uneasy veneer of defiance that quickly crumbled under his intense gaze. And as soon as Ken noticed the change in Matthews' expression, his fist shot out with lightning speed. The force behind it was fueled by pent-up bitterness and struck with the power of a hammer. The impact sent Matthews staggering backward, his head snapping back from the blow to his cheekbone. The sound of bone cracking echoed in the room, making Ken worry that someone might hear it in the hallway. A tooth dislodged from Matthews' mouth and landed on the table amidst a pool of bloody spittle. Blood gushed forth from his mouth, a sickening shade of red that stained everything it touched.

Matthews gasped, a wet, choking sound, struggling to comprehend what had just happened. The blow left him dazed, but the raw violence was even more shocking. "You... you can't do this," he wheezed, the words weak and pathetic, both he and Ken fully aware of how hollow they were. Matthews had sat in countless interrogation rooms over the years, well-versed in the routine. The detective would walk in, drop a file on the table, and maybe throw in some light banter to ease the tension. They'd always say they were there to help, to clear things up, and get his side of the story. Sometimes they got loud, shouted, and made threats—none of which ever fazed him. He knew how to play the game. But this time was different. There was no team of officers, no posturing—just him and Ken. And never before had he been hit.

Again, without warning, Ken threw a punch to his gut. Matthews doubled over in his chair. The pain shot through his solar plexus and into his kidneys. He retched, bile rising in his throat, but nothing came up except a strangled cough. Ken stepped back, giving him a moment to recover and to realize just how much trouble he was in.

"I hope you're understanding the message," Ken asked, his voice cold, detached. He could be discussing the weather for all the emotion he showed. Matthews looked up at him with uneasiness, blood dribbling from his mouth.

Ken leaned in, close enough that Matthews could smell the faint scent of aftershave lingering on his clothes. "You've been given every chance," Ken said, his voice low, a dangerous growl. "And every time, you have spit in our faces. So maybe this visit I'm paying you will help you understand things a little bit clearer."

Matthews shook his head weakly, but Ken grabbed him by the collar, hauling him upright. "Mark my words, I will make you feel what those kids felt. The fear they endured and the pain they suffered. And if you ever go near another child, I'll find you, and I'll make sure you feel it ten-fold." Ken jammed his knee into Matthews' groin sending a searing pain through every nerve in his body. Matthews' body buckled and his legs gave way, but Ken held him upright by his collar and spoke to him just centimeters from his face. "Do you understand?" Vito Matthews nodded his head weakly. "I'm going to need a verbal on that," Ken announced tightening his grip around Matthews' neck.

"Ye…yes." Matthews squeaked out, blood dribbling from his mouth.

The promise was heavy and real. At this point, Matthews was terrified beyond anything he had ever felt. His mind scrambled for a way out, but there wasn't one. Not anymore. He knew this was a line he couldn't talk his way out of, couldn't bribe or blackmail his way through.

Ken slammed him back into the chair, the force of it rattling the metal legs against the floor. He watched as Matthews flinched, and the defiance drained from him, it was replaced with the raw, naked fear that Ken had been waiting for.

At that moment, Ken allowed himself to revel in it - the small sense of retribution with each strike. He finally understood why Weston had asked him to carry out this task. It was a release for Ken, a way to heal and seek justice at the same time. Yet, he couldn't ignore the fact that this wasn't true justice for these vile men, and deep down, he was afraid that real justice might never come.

As he stepped back, his phone buzzed in his pocket, shattering the moment. He pulled it out, glancing at the screen. The name Marchetti flashed across it. Ken's stomach tightened with cold concern. He answered, his voice clipped, "Talk to me."

"They found Mason," Marchetti's voice came through the line, strained, grim. "What's left of him, anyway."

The words hit Ken like a freight train. He barely registered the rest of the call, something about the directions, about getting there as soon as possible. His mind was already racing ahead, trying to piece together what could have happened, what kind of horror Mason had stumbled into.

He hung up, shoving the phone back into his pocket. Matthews was forgotten, a speck of dirt in the larger storm brewing on the horizon. Ken's thoughts were with Mason now, with Grimes, with the creeping, inescapable sense that something far more sinister was at play.

He turned to Matthews one last time, his voice a low, a deadly whisper. "Pray I never see you again, Vito, because if I do, you won't see me coming. " To put a point on the end of his threat, he picked up the tooth off the table and placed it in the top pocket of Vito's blood-soaked shirt. "You dropped this," he said with a smirk and a hard pat on Vito's face.

With that, Ken walked out, the door slamming shut behind him with a final, resounding thud. The precinct outside was a blur of movement and sound, but it barely registered. Ken was already shifting gears, his mind a storm of thoughts as he headed toward the parking lot.

The city towered above him as he stepped out into the world, a vast and apathetic creature. He climbed into his car and immediately spotted a manila envelope sitting on the passenger's seat. With curiosity piqued, he opened it to find his service revolver and a brief note with just two words scrawled in bold letters: "Thank You." And at that moment he knew the envelope was from Detective Weston. He nodded to himself, knowing that while it may have been morally wrong, it was also the right thing to do. The engine roared to life as he drove through the bustling streets with a singular purpose, his car carrying him swiftly toward the scene of the crime like a relentless soldier on a mission.

CHAPTER 5

BLOOD IN THE BUSINESS PARK

The address Marchetti had given him was on the outskirts of town, in one of those desolate industrial areas where the buildings sagged under the weight of years of neglect. It was the kind of place where struggling businesses, on the brink of failure, sought refuge. Hidden from plain sight, tucked away where few would go to venture, it was also a haven for those suspect businesses looking to stay under the radar. When Ken arrived, the area was already cordoned off, police tape flapping in the hot breeze like a twisted banner of death. The squad cars and their flashing lights attracted the attention of curious commuters on their way to or from their otherwise mundane lives.

Ken stepped out of his car, the sun's heat burning through his jacket. He took it off and threw it in the passenger side of his vehicle. As he rolled up his sleeves, he spotted Marchetti near Mason's car, his face pale and drawn. Even from a distance, Ken could see the strain etched into his features, and the way he stood made it look as if he was carrying the weight of the world on his shoulders.

Marchetti's lips pressed into a thin line, and his expression briefly flashed with relief on seeing his partner before hardening with resolve. "It's bad. Real bad."

Ken stepped closer, the unwelcome, metallic scent of blood invaded his senses, sharp and acrid, even though he was some distance from the car. His stomach churned violently, and he instinctively pressed a hand to his mouth and swallowed hard to keep the bile down. He paused, his legs momentarily weak, as the grim reality of the scene hit him with full force.

"You okay to fill me in?" Ken asked, his voice steady despite the turmoil churning inside him.

Marchetti's gaze drifted to the vehicle, his hand hovering mid-air as if he'd momentarily forgotten what to do next. He swallowed hard, the movement slow and deliberate, before speaking again. "It's... I've never seen anything like it, Ken. We're still trying to figure out exactly what the hell happened."

Ken followed Marchetti to the car, his shoes crunched on the gravel beneath his feet. He froze as he took in the scene—blood splattered across the car's interior, congealing in murky, jagged streaks. He locked onto a chunk of flesh caught between the seats, its ragged edges stark against the drying crimson. A sharp, fragmented piece of bone lay on the dashboard, a grotesque reminder of the savage brutality that unfolded.

In the center of it lay what was left of Mason. Or at least, what the detectives assumed to be Mason. The body was unrecognizable. The head was gone, the neck a ragged stump, and the rest of the body was covered in a swath of drying blood. It was as if something had torn him apart with a brutality that defied explanation.

Ken stared at the carnage, his mind reeling. This wasn't just murder—this was something far worse. Something primal, savage. He forced himself to look anyway, to focus on the task at hand. There would be time to grieve later, time to process the loss of a colleague, a friend. But right now, he needed to stay sharp.

"Any witnesses?" Ken asked, his voice hardening as he shifted into work mode.

Marchetti, eyes weary with exhaustion, rubbed them in frustration. "No one has stepped forward yet," he sighed. "A patrol officer stumbled upon him. He noticed the official plates and decided to investigate."

Ken nodded, his disappointment evident.

"But there are… markings, on the headliner. Symbols, maybe but more like writing," Luca said as he pointed out the images just above their heads.

Ken felt a chill run down his spine. The symbols, the brutality, it all pointed to something far more ominous than he had ever encountered. He leaned in closer, getting a better view, of where the symbols had been chalked on the headliner in Mason's car. They were intricate, precise, drawn in Mason's blood with a care that stands in stark contrast to the savagery of the scene. They're not just random marks—they're deliberate, a ritual of some kind. A message, maybe. But for whom?

A chilling memory from a past case resurfaced in Ken's mind, sending shivers down his spine. These symbols were familiar, but where had he seen them before? He searched through his mental Rolodex, recalling every case and horror he had encountered in his years on the force. Only one stood out quite like this one - the first time he had encountered these symbols, he felt the presence of pure evil lingering in the air. The case was unlike any other, with a perverse hatred that seemed to seep into his very being. It wasn't just a crime committed for drugs, money, or passion; it was something far more sinister and calculated, it was killing for killing's sake. "I've seen this before," Ken muttered more to himself than anyone else.

Marchetti squinted at him, incredulous. "When?" He asked, struggling to comprehend that he had witnessed something so rare.

Ken rubbed his temples, as the pieces of that memory started to fall into place. "A few years back, before you joined us, there was a case this... this violent, with writing similar to this. Bodies were found mutilated, and similar symbols were carved into the walls. They were dismissed as cult killings, but no one was ever caught. Eventually, the case went cold."

Marchetti frowned. "Are you sure the writing is the same?"

"Not a hundred percent," Ken admitted, his voice laced with uncertainty. "But whatever it is, it's not just a murder. It's a statement." He said as he traced the symbols with his finger as if it would jog his memory even more. "I've got the cold case files at my desk, we can compare the writing."

The midday sun continued to beat down relentlessly, turning the car into an oven, and baking the blood into the seats. Both Ken and Luca's senses were assaulted by the overpowering smell of death, a fetid odor that clung to their nostrils and throat, making them gag.

"Jesus Christ. Could it get any hotter in here?" Ken mumbled to himself, as he tried to regulate his breathing in short breaths to avoid the full brunt of the stench. Leaning into the car, he forced himself to examine the ragged stump where Mason's head had been. The sight was sickening, the flesh torn and jagged, the wound uneven as if it had been hacked at with something crude and brutal.

A sudden knock on the car window startled the two detectives. Officer Dobbs peered inside and held up a phone for Ken to take. Understanding that it was for him, Ken quickly backed out of the vehicle and accepted the phone from Dobbs. "Thanks," he managed to say with a slight nod. Dobbs nodded back and continued on his way. As Ken raised the phone to his ear, he realized that if he had stayed in the car any longer, he would have been revisiting his lunch for the second time that day.

Luca continued by himself, snapping a few more pictures despite the overwhelming mix of heat and the metallic scent of blood that threatened to make him vomit as well. Each click of the camera felt like a violation, documenting something too vile to be recorded. But it was necessary, a part of the job that had to be done. He paused and examined the frayed skin where the head was severed from the neck. He zoomed in on the image to get a closer look. Then something clicked in his mind. The frayed flesh reminded him of something all too familiar. And it was that thought that almost made him gag.

As quickly as he could, Luca left the car and gulped down the air in huge breaths. It was as if he had been underwater too long. The air outside of the car felt almost sweet in comparison, a stark contrast to the hot death-soaked interior. He took a moment trying to steady himself, but his thoughts were swirling with the implications of what he was piecing together in his head.

Officer Lloyd approached and handed him a small plastic bag. "We found it some twenty yards from the car, Sir," Lloyd explained while Luca quickly examined the macabre piece of evidence in the bag. But his mind was elsewhere.

"Did anyone on the team remove a piece of evidence from the vehicle?" Luca said finally revealing what was on his mind.

"Not that I am aware of, Sir." Lloyd shot back curious to this line of questioning. "Is is something specific?"

"Detective Mason had a large machete in an evidence bag with him," Luca revealed. "It's gone."

Lloyd's expression shifted with surprise. "I've been here since the incident was reported, and I haven't seen anything like that," he reassured Marchetti.

"Keep an eye out," Luca said as he nodded a quick thank you to Lloyd and made his way over to Ken who had purposely gotten as far away from the vehicle as possible without crossing the police line.

Officer Dobbs took the phone back from Ken and returned to Mason's car. "They found the suspect who lost his jacket," Ken informed Luca as he approached. Luca, still dazed, looked up, his mind struggling to process what he was piecing together in his mind. "You okay?" Ken asked, his concern evident.

Luca shook his head, unable to articulate the horror that still churned in his gut. "I've. . . Jesus, this whole thing is horrific," is all he could manage as he handed Ken a zip-lock bag, the gruesome contents inside making his stomach turn.

"They found it about twenty feet from the car," Luca said quietly, his voice laden with discomfort.

Ken stared at it. The skin was bruised and battered, the blood blackened and viscous. He could almost feel the rough texture of it, the violence imprinted in every fiber. "Mason's?" Ken asked, his voice barely above a whisper as if saying it too loudly would make the nightmare more real.

"We're pretty sure," Luca confirmed. "It looks as if someone took a bite out of his face, but they still haven't found… the head. They couldn't find his head anywhere."

The thought made Ken's skin crawl, and a shiver ran down his spine as he imagined the horrific scene that must have played out. He cursed under his breath, his frustration mingling with a growing sense of consternation. "Damn it," he muttered, his fists balling up in helpless anger.

"There's more," Luca said with a sigh.

"Of course there is," Ken replied in frustration."

Luca choked in horror, "I've never witnessed anything like this before." His voice was barely audible as he spoke. "The wound… it looks like it was inflicted with a… Jesus, I can't even say it. It matches the makeshift weapon we discovered on Jane Doe earlier this morning, the one we gave to Mason to put into evidence. It's like they sawed off his head."

"Jesus," Ken replied wondering if they had unwittingly handed over the murder weapon that ended their friend's life.

Both remained silent for a moment contemplating the possibility they may have played a part in Mason's death. Their stomachs churn at the thought.

"Any word on Grimes?" Luca asked, trying to push the thought aside.

Ken shook his head, his thoughts racing. "They're still looking for her. That call was about the kid whose jacket they found in the alley. They have him at the precinct."

"Do you think the blow to her head made her wander off?" Luca's voice wavered.

"I don't know," Ken admitted, his mind reeling with possibilities. Every scenario he imagined was worse than the last, the bleakness of the situation stabbing at him from all sides.

Ken turned abruptly, calling over his shoulder. "Hey, Dobbs!"

Officer Dobbs hurried over, kicking up dust as he approached. "Sir?"

Ken pointed to a building across the way, its blackened windows staring back at him. "Check if those perimeter cameras are working. If they are, get me footage from today."

"Yes, sir," Officer Dobbs replied, turning on his heels and hurrying away, his movements brisk and purposeful. His short stout body made an almost comical waddle as he walked. No one would ever suspect Dobbs for being a police officer if it wasn't for the uniform. He was in his early forties, but his smooth, round face gave him a youthful appearance, a cherubic quality that softened the edge of his job. His skin, a deep, warm brown, glowed with health, and his eyes, large and bright, carried a kindness that contrasted with the sternness expected from the badge on his chest. His smile was infectious, revealing perfect white teeth, and it often disarmed those he encountered, putting them at ease in situations where tension could easily rise.

Dobbs loved his job, he carried his charge with both pride and humility. There was an aura of approachability about him; people were drawn to him, trusting him instantly, whether they needed help or just a friendly conversation. More importantly to the detectives, he was intelligent and a stickler for procedure. Luca and Ken had often put him on the shortlist for a promotion to detective. His eye for detail hadn't gone unnoticed.

Ken watched as he walked away, then redirected his attention to Luca with a serious look on his face. "Let's talk to that kid they picked up."

CHAPTER 6

RITUALS OF DEATH

A couple of miles away from the business park, in a hot and stifling alley, the unbearable heat of the day lingered even as the sun began its descent towards the horizon. The slow breeze whipped up the ripe odor of garbage and rot, the refuse of the city piled high around a sleeping figure. A homeless man, lay on a flattened cardboard box, his shopping cart overflowing with the remnants of a life long since discarded. He slept fitfully, as restlessly as the weight of his despair haunted him even in his dreams.

Seemingly materializing out of the day's unforgiving heat, a figure emerged, moving with a grace that seemed out of place in the filthy alley. The Hag's form was barely discernible as her grey, monochromatic color blended her into the background, her movements fluid and predatory. Her voice was a rasping whisper that broke the stillness, sending a shiver down the man's spine. "Mary, Mary, quite contrary, how does your garden grow?"

The homeless man jolted awake, his body coiled like a spring in a futile attempt to protect himself from the looming figure. He squinted through the blinding light, struggling to focus on the menacing silhouette before him. As his vision cleared, he saw what the figure was holding - Mason's severed head. Pure terror gripped him as the lifeless eyes seemed to scream "Run!" before it fell to the ground with a dull thud, just inches from his face.

But before he could even process what was happening, a resounding THWACK echoed through the alley. The Hag's homemade machete had found its mark in his neck, causing blood to spurt out in a gruesome arc and drenching the walls like a macabre painting. She pressed her foot down on his chest, pinning him in place as she savored every moment of her twisted violence. With each back-and-forth saw of her blade, flesh tore, bones cracked, and an ungodly symphony of savagery filled the air.

The homeless man desperately pawed at the blade, trying to fend off his attacker, but the Hag's strength was unearthly, her movements precise and unyielding. And with one final, sickening THWACK, his head was torn from his body with a gut-wrenching snap. The Hag cackled triumphantly, lifting the severed head by its hair, her putrid breath steaming against the lifeless face. She held it up like a trophy and inhaled the freshly spilled blood. Then, she retrieved Mason's head and continued on her way, her footsteps echoing through the alley as if it were merely a pit stop on a gruesome journey.

***

In the dimly lit hovel she called home, the Hag sat hunched over a rickety table, its surface cluttered with tattered rags, crude medical instruments, and vials of murky liquids. The walls around her seemed to shield her, draped with shadows cast by the light of an ancient hurricane lamp. The weak, sputtering flame barely illuminated the room, yet it was enough for her to see what she needed. Her twisted fingers, gnarled like the roots of an ancient tree, curled around the handle of a rusty straight razor. The blade, nicked and dull, still bore the old stains of past horrors—remnants of deeds too gruesome to be washed away.

For a moment, she paused, her gaze lingering on a tarnished crown that sat in a place of honor atop a crooked shelf. The crown, once resplendent now glinted dully in the hazy light, its luster long since covered in blood, dirt, and grime. Yet, even in its tarnished state, it held a strange power over her, drawing her gaze with an almost magnetic pull.

There was a fleeting moment—a mere blink—where something like sadness glimmered in her eyes, a rare and fragile emotion that seemed out of place in her chilling face. It was as though a memory, long buried beneath the weight of countless years, struggled to rise to the surface. But it wasn't quite a memory; more of a feeling, an echo of something she had once known but could no longer fully grasp. Emotions that had not touched her in what might have been years, perhaps even centuries.

The Hag went numb, and for an instant, she could almost see herself in another time, in another life, wearing that crown not as a relic but as a symbol of power, of destiny unfulfilled. The image was hazy, like a dream fading upon waking, but the sensation it brought was undeniable. She had been someone else once—someone who mattered. The crown had held a promise, not just of authority, but of something far more profound. It had been a beacon of hope to many, a guiding light through the worst of times, and it had given her a sense of purpose.

But as quickly as the feeling came, it vanished, swallowed by the abyss of time and the harsh reality of her existence. The sadness was replaced by cold resolve, the softness of that fleeting moment hardening into the willpower that had kept her alive for so long. Whatever she had been, whoever she had loved, it was gone now—lost to the endless march of years and the cruel twist of fate.

Her objective was clear, the only memory she retained from her past life. It was a wrong that needed to be righted, a mission she had begun while wearing that crown and one that she would pursue for eternity.

With one last look, she returned her focus to the razor, its blade glistening with cold resolve. The fleeting warmth in her heart disappeared, replaced by a fierce determination to complete her task. Fueling herself with this drive, she tightened her grip on the handle, and a nauseating smile formed on her lips.

With painstaking care, she set the severed heads on the table, arranging them as if they were precious artifacts. The dim light glinted off their empty sockets, reflecting nothing but the emptiness that surrounded them. She gazed at the severed heads lined up on the table, her face beaming with a perverse pride. She ran a bloodstained finger across each lifeless face as if tracing the last remnants of their souls. The quivering lamp eerily made the heads appear to nod in silent agreement with her dominance.

These were her offerings—proof of the terror she had sown to honor her master. "Hoc tibi offero, Magister," she mumbled, staring at the arcane writings on the wall. She felt the warmth of their blood coursing through her, a zeal that pulsed in her veins. Each swallow deepened the chasm within her, a pang of gnawing hunger that could never be sated, dragging her further into the abyss. The Hag's hand moved with disturbing precision as she carved another slice of flesh from the homeless man's lifeless face. The blade slid through the skin with a sickening ease, and she lifted the morsel to her lips. Her rotted teeth sank into the meat, tearing it apart with a feral hunger. Blood oozed from the piece and down her chin, dripping onto the table as she chewed slowly, her eyes rolling back into her head in twisted ecstasy.

The Hag's features shifted and contorted, her face now a mask of pure evil. Her expression gleamed with a feral intensity as she savored the last morsels of flesh. The taste of blood and terror lingered on her tongue, a taste that would energize her, giving her the will to continue. With a final bite, she muttered a few words in that ancient, forgotten language, a prayer to the demonic forces that guided her, a plea for more victims to sate her insatiable hunger.

***

On the other side of the tracks, in a forgotten corner of the city, Trent's house stood as a monument to decay, a relic of a time when life held some semblance of normalcy. Now, it was just another part of the city's forgotten landscape, a trailer park where hope had long since withered away. The hallway was poorly lit, the yellowed bulb casting a sickly, pale light over the peeling wallpaper, the floral pattern curling away from the walls like the skin of a snake shedding its old life.

Cheryl Marakakis was still living in that past, a woman whose very existence seemed to defy the passage of time by clinging to every vice, and every poor decision she had ever made, like the moth-eaten house coat she refused to shed. Her body, once perhaps a vessel of promise, had long since surrendered to the ravages of a hard life—a life marked by cigarettes that stained her teeth the color of old parchment and a steady diet of cheap beer that had swollen her frame beyond recognition.

She stood in the narrow hallway of her decrepit trailer, her short, stout body filling the space as if she were a queen surveying her crumbling domain. Her bleached-blonde hair wound tight in the kind of cheap plastic rollers that had seen better days, crowned her head like a mockery of the regality she might have once aspired to. But there was no grandeur in Cheryl, only the remnants of a life misspent, her house dress straining at the seams as it tried to contain the bloated bulk of a woman who had long ago stopped caring about anything beyond her immediate gratification.

The cigarette dangling from her lips was as much a part of her as the wrinkles etched deep into her face, each one a testament to the years of disappointment and bitterness that had settled in her soul like a permanent resident. The ash at the tip threatened to fall, hovering precariously over the threadbare carpet that had seen more burns than it had ever seen a vacuum cleaner. Cheryl's lips pursed as she took a drag, the smoke curling around her head like a shroud, adding to the air of neglect that clung to her like a second skin.

The only light in Cheryl's eyes came from the brief glow of the lighter as she lit another cigarette, the flame reflecting in her cold, blue gaze—a gaze that had long since lost the warmth of hope. Cheryl Marakakis was a woman who had given up long before the world had given up on her. Her son, Trent, was the only reminder of a time when she had wanted more, but even that hope had withered away, leaving behind only the bitterness of unmet expectations and the crushing weight of reality.

As she stood there, staring blankly at the door to Trent's room, Cheryl was not just a woman, but a symbol of everything that had gone wrong. She was a warning, a living testament to the dangers of a life lived without purpose, without care, and without love. As the cigarette burned a long ash that needed to be tapped off, Cheryl simply let it fall, just another piece of her slowly being consumed by the flames of her own making.

Cheryl didn't care. "Boy, get your ass up!" she yelled, her voice rough and raspy, a sound that grated against the quiet of the house. "You're late for school!" She pounded on the door, each thud echoing down the hallway, but the door remained stubbornly closed.

"Leave me alone!" Trent yelled from the other side of the door. His voice was weary and pained.

Cheryl's face twisted in frustration, deep lines carving themselves into her features. "Fine by me," she muttered quietly, her words bitter and edged with the resentment that had been her constant companion for years. "He's eighteen now; it's not my problem anymore. Just like his worthless father," she spat out, turning away from the door. Her footsteps were heavy, the old floorboards creaking beneath her weight as she stalked back down the hallway, leaving a trail of cigarette smoke in her wake.

Inside Trent's bedroom, the feeling was grim, the curtains drawn tight against the daylight, casting the room in perpetual twilight. The walls, once a refuge, now closed in on him, making his sanctuary into a prison. Sweat beaded on his forehead, and his chest tightened as if the air itself had turned against him. He gasped, his fingers clawing at the collar of his shirt, desperate for relief from the crushing weight of his thoughts.

Trent paced back and forth, his movements quick and frantic, like a caged animal searching for an escape that didn't exist. His face gleamed with sweat, his skin pale and slick under the dim light. His left arm was tucked protectively under his right, his fingers digging into his flesh, leaving behind angry red welts.

"Ahhh! Goddammit!" Trent's voice cracked as he shouted, the sound raw and jagged, like something breaking inside him. His pacing stopped suddenly, and he collapsed into the corner of the room, his legs giving out beneath him. He curled up, his body folding in on itself as though trying to disappear, to become as small and insignificant as possible, something that couldn't be hurt.

His chest heaved with the force of his sobs, each one shook his entire frame. The sound of his crying filled the room, bouncing off the walls, and amplifying his despair until it seemed to consume everything around him. There was nothing else—just the rancid air, and the raw, unfiltered pain that devoured him from the inside out.

His fingernails, once neat and clean, were now jagged and bloody, the skin around them torn and raw. Bits of dried blood clung to his fingers, a grim testament to the violence he had inflicted upon himself. The pain was a distraction, a way to keep the deeper horrors at bay, but it was only temporary. The despair was always there, waiting for him to tire, to give in.

Outside the window, the city carried on as it always did, oblivious to the torment happening within those walls. People went about their business, living their lives in blissful ignorance, unaware that just a few feet away, a young man was falling apart, his world crumbling into dust around him. The sun would rise and set, cars would continue to drive past his forgotten part of the city, and the world would keep turning, but for Trent, time had stopped. He was stuck in that moment, trapped in his own mind, unable to move forward, unable to escape the horrors that plagued him.

And in the silence, in the stifling gloom, Trent's mind fractured. He was no longer just a boy in a room—he was a fragment of a soul, lost in a landscape of nightmares, where the walls of reality and horror had merged into one.

CHAPTER 7

CONFESSION

Uniformed Officer Jimenez stood like a statue in the corner of the dimly lit interrogation room, his presence as solid and unyielding as the concrete walls around him. The harsh fluorescent lights above cast stark shadows across his chiseled features, highlighting the lines etched into his face from years of seeing too much. His brown eyes, sharp and vigilant, were trained on the boy sitting at the metal table—a teenager who looked far younger than his years, slumped in his chair with the weight of hours of waiting pressing down on him.

Jimenez's hands were large and calloused from years of service, and rested lightly at his sides. Close enough to his belt to be ready for anything, but relaxed enough to suggest he didn't expect trouble—at least not yet. He had been in countless rooms like this before, with countless people who had the same look of desperation that they didn't fully understand.

Smalls, the teenager at the table, couldn't keep still, his fingers drumming on the cold metal surface as he looked around the room, seeking an escape that wasn't there. He had been waiting for hours, and the tension in his face was palpable, but Jimenez gave no indication that he noticed. He was there to observe, to stand guard, and to ensure that nothing happened until the detectives arrived. And he did this with the kind of quiet, understated authority that came not from words, but from the way he carried himself—like a man who had seen it all and wasn't impressed by any of it.

There was a stillness about Jimenez, a calm that radiated from him even as the boy's anxiety mounted. He had been trained to be the eye of the storm, the center of calm in the chaos, and it was a role he played well. The room felt smaller with him in it, his presence filling the space with a sense of inevitability. Whatever was going to happen, whatever the boy was afraid of, Jimenez would be the silent witness, the one who would see it all and say nothing.

The door swung open with a soft creak, and Ken and Luca entered, their presence commanding, a stark contrast to Smalls' abject misery. Smalls' looked anxiously between Ken and Luca, he wiped his nose with the back of his hand in a useless effort to tidy himself up. He tried to steady his trembling hands, but his breathing became faster, choking his words before they could form. When Ken asked if he wanted a lawyer, Smalls shook his head vehemently, a silent plea in a world that had spun out of his control.

Even without speaking, Smalls knew that Luca and Ken were the ones in charge, the ones who held his fate in their hands. "Where are my parents? I want my parents," he murmured faintly, his voice weak and trembling, barely audible in the heavy silence. Luca grabbed the chair across from Smalls, spun it around, and sat down with a casual posture.

"Happy Birthday, son," Luca said, the words carrying an edge that Smalls couldn't quite place, an undertone that hinted at something more.

"That was two weeks ago," Smalls replied with confusion and tension mingling in his voice.

"Exactly," Ken said, his tone cold and unyielding. "You're eighteen now."

"Mom and Dad are no longer involved," Luca added his words a cold reminder of Smalls' new reality.

Even though his first thought was to have his father help him, somehow Smalls felt a small surge of relief, an instinctive feeling that welled up inside of him. Smalls imagined the look on his father's face, one lined with the marks of middle age, bearing a permanent scowl, the corners of his mouth twisted downward as if frowning had become his natural state.

Despite his mediocre accomplishments, Smalls' father carried himself arrogantly and judged others harshly, including his own son. His expectations were based on his own insecurities, and he desperately tried to assert control over his unremarkable life through his son. Smalls felt crushed by the pressure to meet impossible standards set by someone who had never achieved anything themselves. He knew it was better to face this on his own.

Luca glanced at Ken, and with that silent communication born of years working together, they moved seamlessly into their roles—a well-practiced dance that required no words.

Ken leaned forward, his hands resting on the table as he lowered his voice. "Hey, it's okay," he said, his tone warm, almost like a friend's. "We just want to understand what happened." "What do you like to drink? You got a favorite snack?"

Smalls blinked, bewildered by the mundane questions in the midst of his personal nightmare. "Uh... Twix and Pepsi, I guess."

Luca nodded, handing Jimenez some money. "Get the kid a Pepsi and a Twix," he instructed, his tone casual. Smalls muttered a tearful thank you, his hands shaking as he clung to this small, unexpected kindness—a crack in the dam holding back his emotions.

Jimenez stepped out of the room and closed the door behind him with a thud. His departure broke the tense silence, and Smalls couldn't hold back his tears any longer. He sobbed loudly, unable to control his emotions. Ken and Luca stood by, watching him with heavy hearts. They had witnessed similar situations before - a kid in the wrong place at the wrong time. But this time, something felt different. A sense of foreboding hung in the air, warning them of something they couldn't quite understand.

"Just tell us what happened, and we'll let you be on your way," Ken said, his voice steady, soothing, the promise of safety implicit in his words.

"I'm not in trouble?" Smalls asked, between sobs, disbelief coloring his tone, hope wavering faintly in his eyes.

"Was what happened your fault?" Luca countered, his tone almost fatherly, a gentle prod towards the truth.

"No," Smalls muttered, shaking his head as more tears fell.

Ken leaned in closer; his voice dropped to a near whisper. "Look, kid… we just need to know what happened. Help us out here, and I guarantee that you will walk out of here today."

Smalls inhaled deep, his voice trembling with anxiety and guilt. "I was stupid," he began, wiping at his tears with the back of his hand. "It was Trent's idea to go there. After school, he and Jordy kept talking about the abandoned buildings over on East Avenue. They said it would be fun, you know, like an adventure or something. I… I didn't even want to, but they wouldn't let up. They kept saying I was too scared, that I was a baby if I didn't come with them."

His voice quivered, the memory weighing heavily on him. "So, I went. I thought, maybe if I just went along, they'd stop riding me, you know? But when we got there… there was this woman. She was just minding her own business, digging through some trash like she'd been there forever. She looked like she had nothing, just some rags and an old shopping cart full of junk. But Trent… he just lost it. I don't know what came over him. He started poking at her, saying things—awful things—calling her names, laughing like it was some kind of game."

Smalls' hands shook as he spoke, his focus falling to the floor as if he couldn't bear to meet anyone's gaze. "I told him to stop, but he wouldn't listen. He never listened. And then… then she spit at him, and that… it just set him off even more. Like it was some kind of challenge or something. He got so mad. I could see it, like a switch flipped. He started yelling at her, getting in her face, and I—I didn't know what to do. I should have stopped him, I should have done something, but I was just… I was scared too. He was so pissed and started complaining about his hand, saying it felt like her spit was acid or something. So he started chucking rocks at her. One hit her square in the head, and she fell. That's when we ran."

His voice broke, and he clenched his fists as if trying to hold himself together. "It was all supposed to be just a stupid dare, just some dumb thing to do after school. We weren't supposed to hurt anyone. But Trent... he couldn't let it go. And now... now, everything's gone wrong." Smalls' words caught in his throat, his voice trembling as he struggled to continue. His hands twisting in his lap. "I tried to convince them to leave her alone, but they wouldn't listen. They never listened to me," he repeated, his voice small and faltering.

"Do you know where Trent lives?" Luca asked, his tone probing, seeking the truth behind the fear.

Smalls nodded, and Luca handed him a pad and pen. With trembling hands, Smalls scribbled down the address, the paper shaking as he wrote. A knock at the door broke through the tension, drawing their gaze. Officer Jimenez entered, holding a Pepsi and a Twix bar, setting them on the table in front of Smalls and took his post in a corner of the room.

"Thank you," Smalls said quietly, tearing into the Twix bar with the desperation of someone who hadn't eaten in days. The simple act of eating seemed to offer him some comfort, a brief reprieve from the nightmare he was living.

Ken popped open the soda and set it in front of Smalls, exchanging a glance with Luca that spoke volumes. The reality of their situation sank in deeper, each detail another weight on their conscience. Smalls guzzled it with the same desperation he ate the candy bar, drinking it down as if it were the only thing keeping him grounded.

Luca watched as Smalls gulped down the Pepsi, his brow furrowing. "Take it easy, kid," he said, his voice softening as he reached out to steady the can. "No rush."

Smalls pulled back, nodding as he set the can on the table, his fingers fiddling with it nervously. "Where were we?" Ken asked, his tone conversational, almost friendly, trying to ease Smalls into the rest of the story.

"When I saw Trent the next day... man, his hand was messed up. He had it all wrapped up like it was burned or something. He kept saying, 'She did this to me. That old witch... she cursed me.' I didn't believe him at first, but he... he was obsessed. Said we had to go back, make her pay."

"I went along because I thought I could talk some sense into them, but when we got back to the abandoned building, she was gone," Smalls said, his voice barely audible the memory clearly haunting him. "Then he showed it to us, his hand..." Smalls sucked in a huge gulp of air, "it was gross like it had melted, there was only a... a stump."

"We headed down to East Avenue, where all the boarded-up townhomes are. Trent was convinced she was a squatter, and we'd find her there. And we did, in an alleyway nearby."

Smalls shuddered, his entire body shaking with the memory. "I told him to leave it alone, but he was crazy angry. Kept yelling about his hand and how she was a witch. He even brought a can of gas and said that's how you get rid of witches—by burning them."

Ken shook his head, his expression one of disapproval. "Did she say anything to him, was there any sort of argument?" he asked, his voice calm but firm, guiding Smalls through the fog of his angst.

"No, just crazy stuff," Smalls replied, his body rocking back and forth in his chair, his nerves frayed. "Like a nursery rhyme. Nothing that made any sense."

Luca leaned forward, his interest piqued. "A nursery rhyme? Can you repeat it?"

Smalls nodded in the affirmative. "I think it was 'Mary, Mary, quite contrary,'" He said, his voice trembling, each word another piece of a disturbing riddle.

Ken and Luca exchanged shocked glances, the puzzle wasn't quite coming together in their minds but the pieces were more terrifying than they could have imagined.

"What happened after that?" Ken asked, his voice tense, the question heavy with apprehension.

"Jordy hit her hard with a pipe. It was horrible. He hit her so hard I heard her skull crack, and she went down, we all thought she might be dead and then she got right back up like it was nothing. She grabbed the pipe and... slammed it through his mouth and this old woman lifted him off the ground with it. Then Trent doused her with gasoline. I told him to stop... I swear to God I told him to stop," Smalls confessed, his voice breaking as tears streamed down his face.

Luca handed Smalls a handkerchief, and he gratefully accepted it. He nodded in thanks before burying his face in the cloth, using it to wipe away his tears and conceal his shame.

Ken motioned for Luca to join him just out of earshot. They huddled, their voices low and tense. Smalls gobbled down the last bits of his Twix bar and washed it down with the Pepsi.

"Either he's lying, or we've got some seriously weird shit going on," Luca said, his words spilling out rapidly.

"He isn't lying," Ken retorted, his tone grim, the certainty in his voice adding to the mounting disquietude.

"That's what's freaking me out," Luca responded, turning back to Smalls, his mind racing with the implications of what they'd just heard.

"You gonna arrest me? Please, I didn't do it. I tried to stop them," Smalls pleaded, his voice cracking under the weight of his worry.

"No, kid. We're not going to arrest you. A piece of advice though… stay away from friends like these, I don't need to tell you why," Ken told him, his voice calm and convincing. "Where do you live?"

"On Meade Street, next to the park, 1302," he replied almost with a sense of astonishment.

Ken turned to Officer Jimenez. "Make sure Smalls gets home safely," he instructed, before exiting the interrogation room with Luca.

Officer Dobbs caught their attention as they headed towards the precinct exit and flagged them down. "Detectives," he nodded, holding up a dusty video cassette. "I got the surveillance video from the East Side, but there's a problem," he said, a hint of frustration in his voice. "We don't have a player in the precinct for this old tech," he shrugged.

"My office," Luca said, surprising Ken with the suggestion.

"Seriously? You never cease to amaze me, Luca. You're a damn Boy Scout," Ken joked, a smirk tugging at his lips. "Always prepared."

Luca shook his head. "I'm just old, and I've got old stuff lying around," he replied with a touch of self-deprecation, leading the way.

The smell of freshly brewed coffee filled Luca's office, the rich scent a sharp contrast to the tense atmosphere. Ken watched with bated breath as Luca struggled with an ancient VCR, determined to uncover the truth hidden in the grainy footage playing on the dusty monitor.

Images came to life, casting an eerie glow in the dim room. They fast-forwarded through mundane shots until Mason's car appeared, swerving to a stop on the side of the road. It sat there for a few seconds before starting to rock back and forth in a violent struggle. The sudden splatter of blood against the inside of the car window made both detectives jump in their seats, their eyes glued to the screen in horrified silence. A figure stumbled out of the car shortly after, struggling to stay upright.

As they leaned closer, trying to make sense of the distorted figure on the screen, it wasn't clear that it was Grimes. In fact, she looked nothing like Grimes - her face was gaunt and twisted into a menacing snarl, barely recognizable as human. And her outfit - some kind of bizarre rags that added to the surreal horror of the scene.

But it was what she held in her hands that truly made their blood run cold - the missing piece of evidence from Mason's car, the machete covered in what was probably his freshly let blood. In the opposite hand she carried Mason's severed head. They watched in shock as she turned towards the camera, her face gleaming with madness and malice.

"I can't make out who she is," Ken mumbled through gritted teeth, his voice strained with shock and frustration. But even as he pointed at the screen, trying to make out any distinguishing features, it remained too grainy and distorted to reveal anything useful.

"Can you replay that and zoom in?" Ken's voice edged with desperation as he leaned closer to the monitor, his eyes narrowing as if sheer willpower could bring the image into focus.

Luca scoffed, his disbelief tinged with annoyance. "How am I supposed to zoom in on a cassette tape?" he snapped, the absurdity of the request adding to his growing frustration. His fingers hovered over the VCR's clunky buttons, anachronisms in a world of touchscreens and digital clarity.

Ken, undeterred, mimicked the pinching motion of zooming in and out as if he were holding a smartphone instead of staring at outdated technology. His exaggerated gestures drew an eye roll from Luca, who shook his head before grudgingly pressing the rewind button.

They continued watching until Luca stopped the tape at the moment a beat cop came into view, inspecting the vehicle with the methodical approach of someone who had seen one too many crime scenes.

They watched in silence as the officer leaned closer to the car, his hand shading himself, blocking out the bright sunlight to get a better look at the vehicle's interior. The moment that he saw what was inside, his body recoiled, and he turned away sharply, the violent retching a grim reminder of the horror contained within.

"That's when they called it in," Luca said gravely, the weight of the situation settling like a heavy weight over them both. His voice carried the somber finality of someone who knew that what they were about to face was far beyond the ordinary, far beyond the boundaries of what they had been trained to handle.

Ken rubbed his temples, trying to process the sickening images and the implications that came with them. The air in the room seemed to chill with the unspoken trepidation that they were dealing with something far more sinister and far more dangerous than they had initially thought. The fluctuating light of the monitor cast ghostly shapes on their faces, reflecting the rising distress that neither of them could shake.

Luca rewound the tape, then pressed play again, and the footage resumed its grim parade. They both knew what was coming, but it didn't make it any easier to watch. The figure—inhuman in its distorted, jerky movements—emerged from the car, in a nightmare-given form. Ken strained to make out the details, but the figure remained a blur, a shadowy enigma that defied identification.

Whatever they were facing, it wasn't just another case. This was something else, something that would test them in ways they had never imagined. And deep down, they both knew that whatever was on that tape, it was only the beginning.

Ken let out a deep sigh, the enormity of their task settling heavily on his shoulders. "Where the hell is Grimes?" he muttered, his mind racing with possibilities, each one more terrifying than the last. "Did he drop her off at the hospital first?"

Luca shook his head, no. "The time stamp on the video says it was about ten minutes after he left us, and the hospital is in the direction he's driving."

Luca slammed the stop button, the tape screeching to a halt. The room fell silent, the stress unmistakable. The images lingered in their minds, the implications clear but terrifying. They exchanged a glance, a silent agreement passing between them.

CHAPTER 8

MARCHING ORDERS

The morning sun filtered through the tall, narrow windows of the precinct briefing room, casting thin rays of light over the weathered faces gathered in the room. The air hummed with the tension that only comes when something inhuman has been set loose in the world, and the few who know it must rise to meet it. Laura Weston stood at the front, projecting a calm authority that belied the weight she carried on her shoulders. Her posture, ramrod straight. Her green eyes, sharp as razors.

Ken sat off to her right, his elbows on the table, hands clasped in front of him. Beside him, Luca slouched slightly in his chair, his gaze catching Laura's from time to time. Both men looked as if they hadn't slept, and indeed that was the case. A trio of officers—Dobbs, Brice, and Lloyd—filled the seats at the tables in the front row. They were fresh-faced but seasoned enough to know what kind of morning this would be.

"Morning," Laura began, her voice cool but steady. "We have a situation brewing, and I want all of you informed. I know we've been chasing down leads on a series of sexual assaults, domestic abuse cases, and a couple of kidnappings that all point in different directions. I'm sure you are all aware of the incidents that transpired yesterday where we lost one of our own. This is priority number one. The coroner Jennifer Grimes is still missing as well. Until we can figure out where we stand with the investigation, nothing goes out to the press.

The room was still, save for the low hum of the precinct's old ceiling fan, its blades slowly cutting through the tension.

"Officers Dobbs, Brice, Lloyd—you're being assigned to work directly with Detectives Walsh and Marchetti. I want full cooperation of the entire precinct. No questions asked." Her tone made it clear that there wouldn't be any room for dissent. She held their gazes, one by one. "Whatever these detectives need, they get. Understood?"

A murmur of agreement passed through the room, but it was Walsh who stirred the air next. He stood, his movements deliberate, methodical. "We think that yesterday's two incidents might be related, we're just not sure how at this point. Coroner Grimes has a head injury and we believe time is of the essence in locating her." Walsh began, pacing slowly, his hands gesturing slightly as if the words themselves needed space to breathe. "Grimes disappeared somewhere between the East End and Oakwood Business Park, and we think she might be on foot. We've had our division on high alert all night but nothing yet."

His gaze swept across the room, landing on each officer as though he were locking them into a pact. "Go that extra mile, take that extra step, ask that extra question, the smallest detail might be the one to help us find her.

He stopped near Luca, who was leaning back in his chair, arms crossed over his chest, a dark grin barely touching his lips. Luca had a quiet intensity, one that rippled beneath his cool exterior. He nodded slightly, as if to signal that Ken's words were striking the right chord.

"You're going to see things that'll turn your stomach. But you need to stay focused. This isn't just about nailing perps—it's about saving lives. So when you're out there, keep your eyes open. Look for anything out of place. A car parked too long, someone hanging around who doesn't belong."

The room was silent, every officer hanging on his words.

"These crimes are some of the most heinous we've seen in decades. Be vigilant, be safe and follow procedure. Walsh ran a hand through his graying hair, his fingers momentarily pausing at his temple as if massaging the weight of it all.

Laura nodded at Walsh, stepping forward again, reclaiming the room. "This isn't just a routine assignment. We're at the edge of something big, and it's going to take all of us to bring it down. Stay sharp, communicate, and if any of you find something that raises the hair on your neck, you bring it directly to me or to Walsh and Marchetti."

She glanced at the clock on the wall behind them, her tone hardening. "Now get out there, serve and protect."

The officers rose in unison, their movements deliberate and focused as they headed for the door. The tension that had been simmering now felt like a live wire, crackling with the knowledge that the day would bring danger, possibly more than any of them had bargained for.

As they filed out, Laura and Luca's eyes met for a brief moment—without a word she looked at him with an expression pleading for him to stay safe. Luca nodded, he could sense the worry under the stern exterior as he exited the room with Ken.

"Let's see this boy Trent Marakakis," Ken said, his voice firm, and resolute, as he pushed down the the feeling that was haunting him. Luca nodded with weary determination.

CHAPTER 9

REFLECTIONS OF THE QUEEN

The Hag's hideout clung to the city's edge like a scab, its walls sagging under the weight of years of decay. The wooden beams creaked with each gust of wind that forced its way through the cracks. The small, dilapidated row house barely held itself together, its crumbling walls and faltering roof on the verge of collapse. Faint rays of sunlight struggled through the grime-caked windows, their sickly yellow hue barely piercing the gloom. Dust particles hung suspended in the air, caught in a perpetual dance that gave the room an unsettling sense of frozen time.

The floor was a chaotic mosaic of dirt, grime, and refuse—a testament to years of neglect. Broken bottles, tattered rags, and the remnants of a long-forgotten normal life littered the ground, creating a treacherous, uneven surface that crunched ominously underfoot. Amidst this squalor lay the Hag, her twisted, emaciated form pressed against the filthy floor. Her face, a grotesque mask of gauntness and decay, she was half-buried in the muck as she muttered in a deep gravelly voice.

Her bloodstained lips parted in a rhythmic chant, the words tumbling out like a low, muttering hum that vibrated through the space and then were swallowed up by the dark corners of the room. The air around her trembled bending under the weight of her incantation, as if the very walls were recoiling from the evil she summoned. The sound was hypnotic, a dire chant that mesmerized even as it terrified, an incantation that seemed to warp reality itself. Her gaunt body quaked, her limbs jerking as if pulled by invisible strings, the tremors intensifying until her very bones seemed to rattle. Each spasm wracked her emaciated frame, the sheer force threatening to shatter her from within.

The feeble light filtering through the grimy, cracked windows quivered and distorted, creating eerie images that seemed to writhe and twist with tortured souls. A thick cloud of dust began to swirl, first lazily but then with a mounting speed, drawn into a frenzied dance around the Hag. The light stretched and bent, as if the very fabric of reality was being pulled into the vortex she commanded. Her chanting grew louder, more guttural and urgent, the words spilling from her lips in a torrent of primal power that increased in intensity with each passing moment. The air crackled with raw energy as her voice rose to a fever pitch, driving the swirling dust into a frenzy.

Then, with a blood-curdling scream that tore through the punishing silence, the Hag's body lifted off the floor. She hovered inches above the ground, her limbs contorted and rigid, her head thrown back in a grotesque arc. Her mouth opened impossibly wide, stretching beyond the limits of human anatomy, the skin around her jaw cracking and splitting to reveal the glistening, raw flesh beneath. Memories of hundreds of the innocent burned at the stake flashed through her mind. Their only crime was that they worshipped the same God but in a different way. Her mind drifted back to that time when power was not just a dream but a reality—a time when a different kind of witch held the throne, and the world trembled at her feet.

Once, she was a queen—a ruler whose name was spoken in hushed tones, laced with terror and reverence. She had been born into a world torn apart by the Protestant Reformation, a world where the very fabric of her faith was being unraveled by the hands of men who dared to defy the one true Church. Her father, the great Henry the Eighth, had ripped England from the bosom of Catholicism, casting it into the cold embrace of heresy. And her brother, young Edward, had only tightened the noose around the neck of the old religion, suffocating it with his zeal for reform.

But Mary, she had fought against the tide. She had taken the throne with fire in her veins and a rosary in her hand, determined to bring her country back into the fold of the Holy Roman Church. The Reformation had poisoned her land, but she would cleanse it, even if it meant washing the streets of London with the blood of her subjects.

The memories swirled around her like a thick fog, the faces of the heretics she had burned staring at her with eyes that glowed like embers. They had called her "Bloody Mary," a title she wore with pride, for it was not blood she had spilled, but the very venom of sin. She was purifying England, tearing the Reformation's roots from the soil with her bare hands, even as the people cursed her name.

But the Reformation had not died with the flames she kindled. It had persisted, like a weed growing in the cracks of a forgotten ruin, and when she was laid to rest, it rose again, stronger than before. Elizabeth, her sister and heretic had undone all that she had fought for, casting the realm back into the heresy of Protestantism. Mary's reign had been a brief, furious storm—a tempest that rampaged but could not last. Her passion became a blood lust, and on her death bed she did the unthinkable, she forged a deal with the devil. No longer a quest to have her kingdom under the rule of Rome, now revenge was her only purpose.

The Hag's gaze settled on the tarnished crown that sat upon the table, that relic of a time when she had been more than a whisper in the night. She had been a queen, a force to be reckoned with, and yet now, centuries later, she was nothing but a shadow, clinging to the edges of a world that had moved on without her.

But despite the centuries that passed, the hatred had not dimmed. The fire that burned in Mary Tudor's heart still smoldered within the Hag, fueling her desire for vengeance against those who had betrayed her legacy. The Reformation had taken everything from her, and she would see it undone, even if it took her last ounce of strength. The hunt for heretics, the pyres, the screams of the damned—they were not enough. There was more work to be done, more souls to claim, more blood to spill.

The Hag's lips twisted into a cruel smile as she thought of the boys who had dared to challenge her, who had set her ablaze and thought they could rid the world of her. Fools, all of them she thought. They did not know that fire could not destroy her; it only strengthened her resolve. They would pay for their insolence, just as the Protestants had paid for theirs. The Reformation may have shattered her kingdom, but in this miserable corner of the world, the Hag still reigned.

She would make them all remember. The Reformation had birthed her rage, and it would fuel her until the last drop of blood was spilled. The fires would burn again, and the world would tremble before her wrath. Mary Tudor, the queen who had once been called "Bloody Mary," lived on in the Hag, and her vengeance would be absolute.

Her scream was a sound born of pure agony and indignation, a keening wail that echoed through the row house and beyond, carrying with it the weight of countless tormented souls. The very air seemed to vibrate with her pain, the force of her cry causing the windows to rattle in their frames, threatening to shatter under the strain.

As she hovered, her body convulsed with violent spasms, each shudder sending ripples of corrupt energy through the room. Her eyes snapped open, glowing with an unnatural, wicked light, her gaze fixed on some unseen point in the past, as if communing with forces beyond the human realm.

For a brief, harrowing moment, the world seemed to stand still, waiting with anticipation for some unspeakable event. Then, with a final, wrenching scream, the Hag's body crashed back to the floor with a bone-jarring thud. The dust settled slowly, the sunlight returning to its weak, indifferent glow as if the terror that had just unfolded was nothing more than a passing breeze.

She lay motionless, her body spent from the exertion of her perverse ritual. Her chest heaved, the rise and fall of her ribcage barely visible under the tattered remnants of her clothing.

***

Ken slid into the driver's seat, the engine roaring to life as he held the steering wheel and shifted the car into gear. Luca sat beside him, his gaze fixed on the road ahead, already lost in thought. On any given day his mind would have taken him to his past. The few short years in the priesthood where he would serve as a pastor and then inevitably to his ex-wife. Two of the most important things to him that never worked out and he would ponder the reasons why. But today his thoughts pried at the enigma before them. There were clues and he wondered how they all fit.

They didn't speak, the silence between them heavy with unspoken doubts and unvoiced thoughts. The road stretched out before them, leading them deeper into the bowels of the city, deeper into the unknown, where the line between reality and nightmare blurred, and the only certainty was that everything they believed they knew was now open to question.

The GPS droned on, its mechanical voice a stark contrast to the bleak thoughts swirling in their minds. Finally, Ken broke the silence, his voice low and heavy. "What's going on in your head?"

Luca's focus remained fixed on the road ahead, his mind struggling to process the events that defied all reason. "I don't know, Ken. None of this makes any sense. It's like we're dealing with something out of a nightmare."

The GPS led them into a mobile home park, a place that existed in a strange limbo between temporary shelter and permanent residence. The homes, not quite trailers but not much more, were a patchwork of repairs and additions, a desperate attempt to hold together lives on the brink of collapse. The roads were narrow, cracked, and lined with weeds that pushed their way through the asphalt, a reflection of the decay and neglect that pervaded the park.

As they drove slowly through the park, the sun dipped below the horizon, and the homes, bathed in the dim, fading light, took on an almost sinister appearance. Ken noticed children playing in the dirt, their laughter oddly muted, as if even they sensed the underlying gloom that hung over the place. In the distance, dogs barked, their voices mingling with the hum of old air conditioners struggling against the evening heat.

They finally pulled up in front of the address provided by Smalls. The mobile home was barely distinguishable from its neighbors, a dilapidated structure with peeling paint and sagging steps. The small yard was littered with broken toys and rusted tools, the tiny patch of grass long dead and turned to brittle straw.

Ken turned off the engine, and they both sat in the car for a moment, gathering their thoughts, the weight of what they might find pressing down on them. "Ready?" Ken asked, glancing at Luca.

Luca nodded, his expression resolute. "Yeah."

They stepped out of the car, the gravel crunching under their feet as they approached the front door. Ken knocked, the sound echoing through the rundown house, causing Cheryl to stir from her nap. She sluggishly got up from the couch, a cigarette still dangling from her mouth, her expression one of wary suspicion. "Who the hell?"

Cheryl cracked the door just wide enough for the chain to stretch taut. "What do you want?" she asked, her voice laced with annoyance and suspicion. The stale smoke on her breath mingled with the faint scent of alcohol, drifting into the faces of the two detectives as they caught the sour whiff.

Ken flashed his badge. "Detectives Walsh and Marchetti. We're looking for Trent Marakakis. Is he here?" he asked, his tone authoritative yet non-confrontational. Cheryl hesitated, glancing over her shoulder into the dim interior of the mobile home, the question one she'd been asked too many times before. "Truant?" she asked, her tone implying she already knew the answer.

Ken and Luca nodded without hesitation, relieved they wouldn't have to explain the true reason for their visit—especially to Cheryl, who was anything but accommodating. She closed the door, unlatched the chain, and swung it open wide, allowing the detectives to step inside.

"His room is down the hall," she said, her raspy voice flat, as if leading strangers to her son's room was just another mundane task.

They followed her inside, the smell of stale air and cigarette smoke immediately assaulting their senses. The living room was cluttered, filled with mismatched furniture and stacks of old newspapers. A television blared in the corner, its noise competing with the incessant buzzing of a fly trapped somewhere in the room.

Cheryl led them down the narrow hallway, the walls lined with faded wallpaper and photos of better days. The smell of mold and rot became more overbearing with each step as if they were descending into a root cellar after a hard rain. "Have at it. He's a bum just like his father," she said apathetically as they reached a door at the end of the hall.

She turned and straightened a dusty macrame hanging on the wall as if to make a statement that she was actually a good housekeeper. "Just don't mess anything up," she then added, before shuffling back to her cigarette-burned sofa chair.

Ken and Luca shared a look of disbelief. They couldn't believe she actually said that.

Ken knocked on Trent's door. "Don't mess up the chateau," Luca mouthed dryly. Ken smirked in response, then tried the handle, finding it locked. He knocked again, louder and more forcefully. "Police, open up," Ken barked, the order echoing through the narrow hallway. The sound of rustling came from inside the room. "Come on, Trent, don't make us break down the door. God knows we don't want to piss off your mother."

With a quick, practiced motion, Luca pulled a pen from his pocket, his fingers moving with the precision of a surgeon. He unscrewed the barrel, exposing the thin metal tube inside, then slid the ink cartridge free, leaving just the hollow casing. With a slight twist, he inserted the makeshift tool into the lock, feeling for the pins inside the mechanism. His mind focused in concentration, Luca manipulated the pen with the ease of someone who had done this a hundred times before, carefully applying just the right amount of pressure until he felt the telltale click of the pins aligning.

Ken watched, momentarily taken aback by yet another skill he didn't know the ex-priest possessed. The realization hit him that Luca was far more than he appeared—a man of secrets and unexpected talents. As Luca gave the door handle a gentle turn, the lock released with a soft click, the door yielding to his expertise. Ken, snapping back to the task at hand, quietly drew his service revolver, nodding to Luca in silent acknowledgment.

Luca shoved the door open with a firm push, the wood creaking on its hinges as Ken stepped inside, his gun raised and ready. He swept the room, every corner, every shadow, as he led the way, his senses on high alert for whatever awaited them within.

The sight that greeted them was a tableau of unimaginable horror. Trent huddled in the corner of his room, his back turned to them, a grotesque figure trying desperately to hide itself from the world. The men were hit with the nauseating aroma of decay, mingling with a scent far worse—an odor that spoke of corruption beyond the natural order. As they approached, the reason for the smell became horrifyingly clear: Trent had collapsed against the wall in a corner of the room. His face glistened in the filtered light.

Luca stepped over to the room's window and pulled back the curtain revealing an even more gruesome sight than initially thought. Trent's face was partially melted, revealing raw, bloody flesh beneath. Ken choked back bile. His pulse was practically beating through his neck as he cautiously reached out to comfort Trent. "We're going to get you to a hospital, just hang in there kid." The closer he got, the more the full extent of Trent's injuries came into focus. Ken gently turned him around, his breath catching in his throat as he saw the state of Trent's arm—skin hanging in tatters, the muscle beneath exposed and torn. Then without warning, Trent convulsed violently, his body wracked with spasms. Ken tried to hold him steady but as he grabbed Trent's arm, a chunk of it slid off in his hand and onto the floor. Abruptly, Trent retched, vomiting a foul, black liquid that splattered all over Ken's shirt before finally, mercifully, succumbing to his injuries.

"Jesus Christ," Ken muttered, his voice trembling with shock and horror. He stepped back, fighting the urge to be sick, the grotesque reality of the situation clawing at his sanity. "What the hell happened to him?"

Luca, equally shaken but maintaining a facade of calm, knelt beside Trent, scanning the room for any clues that might explain the nightmare they'd stumbled into.

He checked the pulse on Trent's outstretched hand, his face a mask of concern and revulsion as he tried not to touch the pus-filled boils festering on every inch of Trent's body. "It's like he melted from the inside out," Luca explained, using the same pen he used to pick the lock to push away a flap of skin, revealing the putrid tissue beneath.

Unable to bear the stench any longer, Ken hurried to a nearby chest of drawers, rummaging through it for a clean shirt. The overwhelming odor, a nauseating blend of decay, and something far more sinister assaulted his senses.

"What are you doing?" Luca asked, noticing Ken's frantic search.

"I can't take this smell," Ken replied, holding up a Metallica t-shirt that was clearly too small for him, his face pale and sweating. "I've got to take this off," he continued, pulling at his soiled shirt in frustration.

Luca, his voice steady despite the chaos, spoke into his radio. "Dispatch, we need immediate assistance. Send a CSI team to our location and a body wagon. We've got a situation here."

The radio crackled in response, and Luca turned to Ken, his expression grim. "There's something else at play here. Something we don't understand."

Ken nodded, his mind racing with possibilities, none of them comforting. "We need to figure out what did this to Trent. And fast."

As they turned to leave the room, a low moan echoed through the room, freezing them in place. Ken and Luca turned towards Trent's lifeless body, the sound emanating from deep within his chest—a final, haunting exhalation that sent chills down their spines as Trent's body melted into a pile of flesh right in front of them. All that was left was a pile of flesh with the occasional bone sticking out of it.

"What in God's name?" Ken gasped. "Can we get the hell out of this room before I wretch?" Ken said, holding back the vomit rising up in his throat.

"What about her?" Luca asked, nodding in the direction of the living room, where Trent's mother remained oblivious to the carnage just feet away.

"As soon as CSI gets here, we'll let them deal with it," Ken replied, his tone without a hint of any guilt, his focus solely on getting out of that room as quickly as possible.

As they stepped out of Trent's room they walked quickly past Cheryl as she took another drag from her cigarette, staring at the grainy images on her ancient television set, lost in a world of apathy and denial. The scene was surreal, the two detectives felt as if they were walking in slow motion through a bizarre dream. There in front of them was the grotesque clown of Trent's mother, oblivious to the horror just feet from her as she belly laughed at the pathetic antics of guests fighting on the Jerry Springer show. Maybe in some small way, she believed she was better than them, and maybe she was, for all her faults, at least she didn't air her ignorance in public.

A siren whined just outside of the trailer. "Thank God, they're here," Ken thought to himself.

"We've got some colleagues here to help out, " Luca said, his tone not giving away any indication of the enormity of what she was about to face.

"Yeah, whatever," she replied nonchalantly, waving her hand in a dismissive gesture. "Just remind them to wipe their feet before they enter my house." And with that statement, she perfectly summed up the strange reality they were currently living through.

Ken and Luca emerged into the desolate night, their minds heavy with the weight of the unknown. He motioned to the EMTs who had already exited their ambulance and were preparing their equipment."It's in the back, at the end of the hallway," Luca stated flatly, masking the horrors that awaited them in that small corner of Hell. There was no way to prepare them for what they would find inside, so without another word, the detectives climbed into Ken's car and drove off into the darkness, which seemed to whisper of even more terrifying things yet to come.

CHAPTER 10

STALKED BY SHADOWS

Ken, Luca, and Mitch, the coroner, gathered in the sterile white room around a metallic table covered with a pristine sheet. Mitch wore a pressed white lab coat and his thick glasses rested on the bridge of his nose as he leaned in to examine the charred remains beneath the covering. His face showed disbelief at the scene before him: instead of a body, there was only dust and debris. The air in the room was dense with the smell of antiseptic, covering up any other odors that may have lingered from the tragic event. A solemn hush fell over the trio as they tried to comprehend what lay before them.

The fluorescent lights overhead made Mitch look more stern than he actually was, deepening the lines etched by years of worry rather than wisdom. He was a man who had spent his career in the shadow of those more competent, more confident —coroners like Grimes, whose precision and expertise had made her a legend in the morgue. But Mitch was no Grimes.

Where Grimes had been meticulous and unflinching, Mitch was hesitant and uneasy, his every movement betraying the doubts that gnawed at him. The white lab coat he wore hung awkwardly on his short slouched frame, as if it didn't quite belong to him, much like the title of coroner that he had somehow acquired but never fully owned.

But it wasn't just his skill that fell short; it was his very presence in the morgue. Grimes had commanded respect, her mere presence in the room enough to silence any doubts. Mitch, on the other hand, seemed to invite them. His voice, when he spoke, was soft and uncertain, lacking the authority that had come so naturally to his predecessor. Even now, as he addressed the detectives, his words were laced with hesitation, as if he were constantly seeking validation, reassurance that he wasn't about to make a fool of himself.

As he pulled back the sheet revealing the space where a body should have been, Mitch's heart sank further into the pit of his stomach. The mistake wasn't his, but it felt like it. He could almost hear Grimes's voice in his head, pointing out the obvious, catching the details he might have missed. But she wasn't there to guide him, and Mitch was left alone to face the unsettling reality of his own inadequacy.

"I swear I was only gone for two minutes," Mitch hesitated, his hand trembling slightly as he gripped the sheet.

"You didn't see anyone come in or out?" Luca's tone was sharp and urgent, as his eyes scanned the room for any sign of intrusion. He snapped on a pair of latex gloves.

Mitch shook his head, his troubled frown deepening. "Why would anyone want to steal the remains of a Jane Doe?"

"That's what we're trying to figure out," Luca replied as he processed the bizarre situation.

Luca took the corner of the sheet from Mitch and lifted it noticing the greasy, ashy smudge where the body should have been. He swiped at the greasy residue and rubbed it between his fingers. "What is this?" He thought. "It's not just dirt left behind from the charred body that was once lying here."

Ken shivered involuntarily, the chill from the metal table seeping through his gloves as he gingerly lifted the sheet at the other end, his gaze settling on a lone toe tag where the feet should have been. He picked it up, examining it closely, his expression grim. The tag showed the name as "Jane Doe," and included the date of death, a case number, the cause listed as "pending," and the cold reminder of the morgue's facility number beneath the words "Unknown Female." "Nobody stole her," he announced, his voice heavy with the weight of realization.

Mitch looked at him incredulously. "Well, she certainly didn't just get up and walk out of here," he retorted, the absurdity of the situation obvious.

"And no one would waste time removing the toe tag if they were in a rush," Ken added, holding up the tag as if it were a crucial piece of evidence in a puzzle that refused to make sense.

Mitch stood awkwardly silent, fidgeting, and unsure of what to do next. Luca raised a hand, gesturing for him to wait outside. "Could you give us a second?" After a moment's hesitation, Mitch exited, leaving the two detectives alone in the eerie stillness of the morgue.

Once Mitch was gone, Luca stepped closer to Ken, his jaw set, and his eyes locked onto his partner's. "There's something I need to tell you," he said, his voice low and firm, every word carrying a weight that made Ken pause. He exhaled hard as if steeling himself for what he was about to reveal.

"You remember I used to be a priest, right?" Luca's voice dropped, each word measured as he searched Ken's face for a reaction. Ken tried to lighten the mood. "Yeah, yeah, it's your go to pickup line when you're drunk," he joked, a smirk playing on his lips.

But Luca's expression remained grave. "Did I ever tell you why I left the priesthood?"

Ken shrugged, the smirk fading as he sensed the seriousness of the moment. "I don't know, the pay sucked? Or maybe you wanted to get laid like the rest of us."

Luca nodded toward an empty table in the corner of the room, his gaze distant, as if seeing something that wasn't there. "Because of shit like that," he said grimly.

Confusion crossed Ken's face as he followed Luca's gaze to the empty table. "Like what?"

Luca hesitated, the memories painful. "I assisted on an exorcism once, fifteen years ago," he said, his voice low, intense. "I had taken the required courses to be an exorcist, still trying to find my place in the Church, and I figured what the hell, let's see what it's all about. My instructor in Rome, Father Amorth, was an eccentric but brilliant teacher, and of course, on day one, the questions were probably always the same, "Had you ever seen someone levitate? Was it like in the movies?" And so on. He would smile knowingly and say, 'I will teach you how to fight against evil first, then I will answer your questions. If I answer them now, you will leave and never come back.'"

Luca's voice caught for a moment, his gaze clouded with the memory. "It was a young girl, around twelve years old. She reminded me so much of your daughter - kind, lovely, intelligent - but inside her lurked an ancient demon that had roamed the Earth for centuries. And right in front of me, this innocent child transformed into a nightmarish creature. Her skin shriveled, her fingers twisted into claws, her once black hair turned stark white, and her teeth sharpened into knives... the angel had become a monster."

Ken shook his head, disbelief etched into his features. "Seriously? You know what drugs can do to a person, it was most likely just some crazy woman high on bath salts."

"No. I saw that kid," Luca insisted, his voice fierce, filled with a conviction that sent a shiver down Ken's spine. "That twelve-year-old little girl transformed into an 80-year-old reflection of wickedness and that was more than I could handle. The thought of that type of evil made me feel powerless."

Realization dawned on Ken's face as he connected the dots. "Wait… the woman who attacked Mason in the video… that's Grimes?"

"Was Grimes," Luca confirmed gravely. He pointed to the exam table. "You're right, nobody stole her body. It up and disappeared just like that," he emphasized by snapping his fingers.

They both fell silent, the weight of Luca's revelation settling heavily in the room. After a moment, Ken spoke again, his voice tinged with uncertainty. "You're serious?"

Luca met his gaze, nodding solemnly. "I wish I wasn't."

***

Rain pounded against the windowpanes of Luca's dimly lit apartment, the rhythmic drumming a stark contrast to the quiet concern inside. The small desk in the corner was cluttered with hastily scribbled notes, an open police file, and a laptop glowing with pale light. Luca sat hunched over the screen, reading across the lines of text as he sifted through website after website, piecing together fragments of a disturbing puzzle.

"What exactly are you searching for?" Ken asked, trying not to disturb Luca's focus. He peered over Luca's shoulder. The only source of illumination was the computer screen and the occasional burst of lightning outside.

"This," Luca answered placing his finger on a picture in Ken's cold case file. "The symbols you mentioned in your cold case. Now do these look familiar," Luca asked pointing to the screen that read "אנא יהיב לך נקמתא."

"It matches the picture and the writing we saw on the headliner of Mason's car," Ken said incredulously. "What is it?"

"Aramaic," Luca responded not believing what he was saying.

"A language?" Ken asked.

"Yeah, Galilean Aramaic, to be specific. The language of Jesus. Not a widely known language today, especially in this form," Luca explained.

"Can you decipher what it means?" Ken asked.

"I've been matching up the letters with a dictionary here online. As best as I can tell, it reads, 'I offer you my vengeance,'" Luca said, as he followed the symbols with his index finger one by one. "Then there is this," Luca flipped to another website that chronicled the reign of Queen Mary I, known as "Bloody Mary." "Somehow this is all linked, I just have no clue how."

Ken leaned in further, his brow furrowing as he scanned the text. "I'm not following," he admitted, shaking his head in confusion. The historical references felt distant, disconnected from the horrors they were currently facing.

Luca sat back in his chair, his gaze fixed on the screen as if he could force the connection to reveal itself through sheer willpower. "This is what keeps bothering me. There's a connection, but it's just out of reach," he explained as he pointed to the screen, his finger hovering over a line of text. "Read what it says here."

Ken obliged, his voice tinged with skepticism as he read aloud. "Mary Tudor, Queen of England from 1553 to 1558, tried to reverse the Protestant Reformation by executing hundreds of people," His voice trailed off, his mind struggling to see how this historical context fit with their current case.

Luca nodded, his expression thoughtful as if he were on the verge of a revelation. "This is the origin of the nursery rhyme. 'Mary, Mary quite contrary'—it's said to be a metaphor for her bloody reign. 'Silver bells and cockle shells' represent instruments of torture, and 'pretty maids all in a row' refers to her executions. And the Aramaic refers to "offering vengeance," Somehow they're connected. But how?" Luca explained as he tried to wrap his mind around the clues that seemed to float just out of grasp in his mind. "She burned heretics at the stake, around three-hundred of them," Luca added. "Trent's wounds. The boils, the skin practically melting off of him, it was as if he was burned without the scarring."

His phone buzzed and without hesitation, he snapped the laptop shut as if he didn't want the caller to see what they had discovered. With a curt tone, he answered the call. "Marchetti," he stated sharply. He listened intently, his brow furrowing as the person on the other end spoke. Finally, he hung up, his gaze meeting Ken's with a fierce resolve. "That was Dobbs," Luca said. "They think they found the perps' place off East Avenue."

They rose in unison, the urgency of the situation pushing them into action. Their senses were on high alert and stress levels peaked as they feared a terror yet to come. They grabbed their jackets and headed for the door. Without hesitation, they stepped out into the stormy night, the rain immediately soaking through their clothes as they hurried to the car.

Ken drove as the rain pelted the windshield, his thoughts consumed by a million questions. The headlights bore through the storm, but the shadows that surrounded them felt alive as if they were closing in with every passing second.

After a long silence, he spoke up, his voice tense. "Listen, Luca, I find it hard to believe any of this. But let's just say, for argument's sake, that you're right. What could that possibly be?"

Luca's weary and anxious eyes flicked toward the rearview mirror as if expecting something terrifying to appear at any moment. "Look at Grimes," he said with a strained voice. "She displayed all the signs, but I didn't pick up on them."

Ken furrowed his brow in skepticism, deepening the lines on his face. "What signs? Possession?" His words hung heavy in the air, laced with disbelief, but the uneasiness in Luca's voice was hard to ignore.

"The final stage of possession," Luca replied grimly. "Complete control by the entity."

The word "entity" echoed in the car, sending a chill down Ken's spine. The reality of their situation was starting to set in, but he wasn't ready to accept it.

Luca went on to explain the signs he had missed. "First, self-harm. Then she knew things she couldn't have known, like that Latin phrase. And did you see how strong she was? She flung Mason aside like he was nothing."

Ken nodded slowly, recalling Grimes' unnatural strength. He had heard stories of drug addicts on PCP displaying extraordinary strength, but he knew that couldn't be the case with Grimes. "But couldn't it all just be adrenaline? And maybe she saw the rhyme written somewhere or it was just a coincidence," Ken suggested, grasping for rational explanations.

Luca nodded absently, his mind replaying the frightening scene over and over again. "It could all be chalked up to adrenaline or coincidence," he agreed. "But the Latin..."

Ken squinted, trying to remember what Grimes had said in those chaotic moments. He shook his head, then paused. "Yeah, she was just babbling nonsense, I couldn't understand a word."

"Habebō vindictam meam," Luca's voice was barely audible, as if speaking the words could summon something demonic.

Ken perked up at the phrase, realizing it sounded familiar. "Wait, but doesn't she know some Latin?"

"Some medical terminology would make sense, but 'Habebō vindictam meam'?" Luca replied.

"What does it mean?" Ken asked, unsure if he really wanted to know.

Luca's face paled and his lips barely moved as he spoke. "I will have my vengeance."

The phrase lingered in the air like a chilling promise from an unseen force. The pieces of the puzzle were starting to come together with horrifying clarity as they realized the true nature of their situation. The Aramaic, the Latin, it all fit.

"Fuck. Smalls! He's in danger." Luca's eyebrows lifted, the realization hitting him like a punch to the gut. "Damn it, how could I have missed that?!"

"Shit!" Ken blurted out, the same realization dawning on him.

Ken slammed on the brakes without warning, the car lurching violently as the tires shrieked against the asphalt. The vehicle skidded to a bone-jarring halt in the middle of the road, the world outside blurring into a whirl of lights. As Ken spun the wheel with determined fury, Luca braced himself in the passenger seat, one hand gripping the dashboard, the other clutching the edge of his seat. The oppressive night pressed in on them, the headlights slicing through the rain, while Luca's mind raced to piece together their next move, knowing that whatever came next would demand everything they had.

The road ahead seemed murkier than ever, the headlights carving a narrow path through the night. As they sped toward Smalls' house, their minds raced, not knowing just what they'd encounter.

CHAPTER 11

THE HUNT

The wind howled through the streets, whipping the rain into a frenzy that lashed against windows with relentless force. Lightning split the sky, illuminating the twisted branches of trees bent over by the gale, while thunder rumbled like the growl of some unseen beast. A lone streetlight shimmered weakly, casting a feeble glow over a small patch of desolate road. The night was dense, like an oppressive cloud that seemed to swallow the world whole.

From the inky shadows, a figure emerged and stepped into the pale circle of light. The rain hammered against her hunched silhouette. With a calculated pace, she moved closer to Smalls' house, her tattered cloak flapping in the wind and dripping with oily water. A foul stench surrounded her, like a putrid cloud of malevolence that oozed from her ragged frame. She paused at the edge of the light, sniffing the air like a predator on the hunt. Then, with a fierce hunger in her gaze, she continued forward, savoring each step as if relishing the terror she instilled in those around her. It was the Hag, and she had come for Smalls.

The Hag's hand gripped the machete that caught the light in a sickly crimson and black sheen. She moved with the fluid grace of a predator, each step bringing her closer to her prey.

The gentle light from the nightlight softly illuminated the walls in Smalls' room. They were adorned with posters of his favorite movies and idols who he dreamt of emulating one day. As he slept soundly in his bed, he was completely unaware of the turmoil brewing just outside his bedroom. At that moment, he was simply a teenager, cocooned in his own peaceful haven.

But outside, just beyond his window, the Hag crept closer. She moved like a wisp of smoke in the breeze, her footsteps silent and purposeful. Each step brought her nearer to the house, to the unsuspecting boy within. The night was her ally, cloaking her in its depths as she advanced, the machete a perverse promise of violence.

Inside, Smalls stirred slightly, turning in his sleep but not waking. The nightlight quivered momentarily as if even the light itself was afraid. With his earbuds in, a faint and haunting melody leaked out, barely breaking the quiet that hung like a shroud over the room. The music, once comforting, now seemed to fade into the night, a ghostly whisper against the storm.

Without warning, a deafening boom of thunder split the silence, rattling the windowpanes and shaking the very foundation of the house. Lightning followed a sharp crack that illuminated the room in a harsh, unnatural bluish-white light. And in that brief, terrifying flash, Smalls' eyes snapped open.

A face appears—twisted and grotesque, a nightmare made of flesh. The Hag, her ancient and vile presence overwhelming, stood at the foot of his bed. Her face was a ghastly mask of decay, as she stared at him with venomous intent. The sight was so sudden, so visceral, that it was seared into his mind as the room plunged back into inky blackness.

He gasped as he fumbled for his glasses on the nightstand. With his hands shaking, he finally managed to put them on and scan the room frantically. But there was nothing. The room was as it had been—silent, empty, yet charged with a sinister energy that hadn't been there before.

The rain, which had been a constant drumming on the window, ceased abruptly, leaving an eerie silence in its wake. The only sound now was the wind and music from his earbuds, which had inexplicably grown louder, as if mocking his terror. The melody now creating a discordant symphony that set his teeth on edge.

He could feel the room closing in on him. He tried to keep calm and convince himself that it had all been a dream—a lingering nightmare from that horrific event that would haunt his nights until the very end. But the panic welled up inside him, insistent, refusing to be dismissed.

Another bolt of lightning lit up the room, stark and unforgiving. In that instant, he saw her again—the Hag, her hideous face just inches from his. Her scent, hot and putrid, filled the room with an aroma almost unbearable in its intensity.

"Please, no!" he choked, his voice barely more than a whimper. "I tried to stop them." But his pleas fell on deaf ears.

His breathing grew rapid and shallow as panic set in, the room spinning around him. He was paralyzed, unable to move or scream, trapped in a nightmare from which there was no escape. Her stare bore into him, cold and unfeeling, as if she were savoring his terror, feeding on it. She sniffed the air like a beast evaluating its prey before finally settling on him. In her expression, there was a clear understanding - he was the last one she had been seeking.

Outside, Ken's black sedan pulled up in front of Smalls' house, its headlights boring a hole through the night. The two detectives emerged from the car, their expressions stoic. Their jaws were tight as they scanned the area, on high alert for any potential danger.

The rain had finally passed, leaving behind a smothering film of moisture. Every surface was coated in shimmering droplets, glinting in the dim light of the lone street lamp and the occasional flash of lightning on the horizon. The air was leaden with the scent of damp grass and the sharp tang of rain on pavement, but beneath it all lay an ominous undertone. A faint, foreboding odor clung to the atmosphere like a warning, a lingering reminder of death lurking just out of sight. It was a smell that would soon become synonymous with terror and dread.

Luca reached for his police radio and spoke urgently. "Send a squad car out to 1302 North Meade Street. Walsh and I are going in."

"Copy," came the crackling response from dispatch, the voice tinged with static.

They moved quickly, knowing there was no time to hesitate, the surreal tone of the night nagging at them, warning them of danger. The distant flashes of lightning seemed to move closer as they approached the house.

"You got the back?" Ken asked, his voice was low, tense.

Luca nodded, disappearing towards the back of the house, his flashlight beam flicking to and fro as he vanished from sight. Ken continued toward the front door, his senses on high alert.

He rapped on the door, the noise echoing through the quiet neighborhood. Then, he repeatedly hit the buzzer with his thumb, creating a jarring melody that could be heard inside the house. As he waited for a response, he scanned his surroundings, catching a glimpse of movement out of the corner of his eye. It was probably just his mind playing tricks on him, but it still sent a shiver down his spine. The video doorbell buzzed loudly, breaking the silence and causing him to jump. A voice blasted through the speaker, startling him even more. "It's late. Who is it?"

Ken quickly regained his composure, holding up his badge to the camera. "Police, Mr. Smalls. We have reason to believe your son Robert might be in danger, I need you to open up now."

"What do you mean, 'danger'?" The voice was wary, still stern but with a mix of confusion and concern.

Ken's frustration grew. The night air was heavy with the scent of rain-soaked earth and the distant rumble of thunder. "Mr. Smalls, please open the door. I'll explain everything."

"He's fine. He's in his room. Come back tomorrow. It's two in the goddamn morning!" The voice from the intercom was irritated, clearly not understanding the urgency.

Ken balled his fists, struggling to maintain his composure. The gravity of the situation weighed heavily on him, each second feeling like an eternity. "We have police backup on the way, Mr. Smalls. This is urgent. Please, open the door."

In his bedroom, Smalls remained frozen in terror, his mind racing to make sense of the terrifying events unfolding before him. His heart thumped wildly in his chest as he tried to comprehend how everything had led up to this moment.

The room was illuminated sporadically by flashes of lightning and the sound of thunder grew louder and closer with each passing second. The Hag's presence loomed over him, oppressive and inescapable. Slowly, she raised a machete, the blade reflecting a glimmer of light that seemed to form a sinister grin. Every movement was calculated as if she were savoring the anticipation of delivering a menacing blow.

As fear overtook him, smalls lost control of his bladder, warm urine soaking into the sheets beneath him. He shook uncontrollably, teetering on the edge of madness. The Hag's hand clamped over his mouth, her grip cold and unyielding, muffling his cries.

Even the night light seemed afraid, fluttering erratically. Smalls tried to scream, but his voice was drowned out by her hand and booming thunder that rattled the walls. Then she froze and stared at him, her face inquisitive as if she were asking herself a question. Unexpectedly, she lowered the blade and set it on his neck. The serrated edges immediately puncturing the skin. And with one swift movement she yanked the blade backwards slicing into his neck. The pain was immediate, and excruciating, but the wound was only deep enough to allow blood to seep out in a steady stream. Smalls bucked in agony, his movements frantic and uncoordinated.

Everything about her, assaulted his senses as she leaned in close, her voice a chilling sing-song as she dug the blade a little bit deeper into his neck.

"Mary, Mary, quite contrary…"

Smalls' vision started to blur, the edges of his world shrinking. The pain was unbearable, each breath a chore. His struggle was useless under her strength. He could feel himself bleeding to death, the room spun as his consciousness faded.

But that wasn't enough. The Hag wanted more, needed more. One of her tormentors deserved so much more than mere decapitation. She laughed, a rotted, gurgling sound, as she hacked away at Smalls' arms, blood sprayed in a warm, sticky arc, splattering against the walls and bedding. One by one, the severed limbs fell grotesquely onto the floor, the scent of blood overwhelming.

"How does your garden grow?" she crooned, her voice dripping with malice, each word a twisted mockery.

The sheets soaked up the crimson liquid that gushed from every wound. With both arms severed the Hag turned her attention to his legs. Smalls' body lay in a pool of his blood, shock, and horror etched onto his face.

The Hag pulled back the machete for another blow, blood still squirting from his arms in rhythmic spurts.

"With silver bells and cockle shells and pretty maids all in a row."

Smalls faded in and out of consciousness, his physical pain had been overshadowed by the shock of witnessing his limbs being amputated one by one. The machete came down again, this time into his other leg, and she began to saw back and forth, her movements efficient and gruesome, a macabre gardener tending to her grim harvest. The room was filled with the sickening sound of metal against bone, and the smell of fresh blood.

As Smalls fell deeper into the endless abyss of his mind, a deafening ringing filled his ears, morphing into a piercing scream unlike any he had ever experienced. The terror seemed to consume him whole and he felt death wrap its cold grasp around his heart. But even as it threatened to suffocate him, he couldn't shake the vivid image of the Hag carving him up like a slaughtered cow. He couldn't help but wonder when he would wake up from the nightmare. And just when he thought things couldn't get any worse, the Hag sneered triumphantly and revealed her rotten, jagged teeth as she swung her merciless blade down onto Smalls' neck. With a sickening crack, his head was separated from his body and rolled to the ground. As his lifeless eyes met the gaze of the Hag, she roared with delight.

Luca rounded the corner of the house to see Ken pounding on the front door. "All clear," he yelled over the whipping wind.

Ken pounded harder, his frustration had boiled over as he yelled into the camera. "His friends, Trent and Jordy are both dead! Please, open up!" He pleaded desperately, his voice cracking with urgency.

Instantly, the door opened, revealing his face with a mask of shock and confusion. "Dead?"

Ken and Luca pushed their way past him, the urgency in their movements obvious. "Where's his room?" he barked.

"Down the hall on the right," Smalls' father replied, his voice trembling barely getting out the words. His bravado was gone, his arrogance taking a backseat to what could only be described as despair.

The hallway light flickered as lightning cracked outside. The detectives rushed through the house, their footsteps hammering on the wooden floor, the smell of damp wood and that strong smell of death growing closer with every step they took.

They reached the door at the end of the hall, the one with a childish "Do Not Enter" sign taped haphazardly onto it. The sight of it was jarring, an out-of-place innocent marker of youth now serving as the entrance to something far more sinister. Ken didn't hesitate. He grabbed the handle and twisted. It was locked.

"Robert!" he called out, pounding on the door. The silence that greeted him was heavy and punishing. He pulled his gun from its holster and took a step back, bracing himself. There was no time to casually pick the lock so he heaved his shoulder hard into the door making it shudder on its hinges. But it didn't give.

"The door!" Smalls' father yelled as he scrambled to meet them. His concern for the door being damaged showed he still had no concept of the danger his son was in.

"Stay back!" Luca's screamed with such ferocity that Smalls' father froze in his tracks.

Undeterred, Ken took another run at the door and this time the wood splintered, bursting open with a loud groan as pieces of it flew into the room. But when he stumbled inside, gun drawn and ready for action, the sight before him caused him to come to a screeching halt. "God almighty," he gasped, taking in the horror that was Smalls.

Without even seeing what had caught Ken's attention, Luca sensed it was something beyond their worst nightmares.

Smalls' father called out for Bobby and rushed towards the room. But Luca stepped in his way, not letting him get close enough to see the horrifying scene that awaited them.

The room was a nightmare brought to life. The smell of blood was overwhelming, mixing with the sweet perfume of rotting flesh. Smalls' bed was soaked in red, the sheets tangled and stained. His body—what was left of it—lay in pieces, grotesquely arranged around the room like some kind of macabre jigsaw puzzle. Arms and legs, all severed with brutal precision, lay scattered on the floor, the room's dim light barely illuminating the carnage.

Ken could scarcely process what he was seeing. His mind reeled, his stomach turning, but he compelled himself to stay attentive. He stepped carefully around the body parts and looked out of the open window. It was the only way out, but there was no sign of anyone—or anything—outside.

"Luca!" Ken shouted, his voice a strained mix of horror and urgency. "Get in here!"

Luca entered, his face went pale as he saw the blood-soaked room and the scattered limbs. "Jesus Christ," Luca mumbled to himself, the words barely escaping his lips. He exchanged a horrified glance with Ken, the reality of the situation sinking in.

Smalls' father rushed in behind him, his face twisted in a mixture of shock and disbelief. He pushed past Luca, frantically searching for his son before he realized only pieces of him were left. His mind raced. Part of him wanted to turn away, unable to bear the sight of what had become of his son, but another part couldn't look away, consumed by a need to understand what had happened.

"Bobby? No... Bobby!" he cried, his voice breaking as he fell to his knees. The man's anguish was palpable, a raw anguish that filled the room.

Ken stepped closer to the window, peering out into the stormy night. The wind howled, rattling the loose panes, and carried with it the scent of rain, blood, and something else—that smell that would haunt him until the end of his days. But there was no movement outside, no sign of the killer.

Luca reached out, placing a hand on the father's shoulder, trying to offer some small comfort. But there were no words for what had happened here. Nothing could make sense of this senseless, brutal act.

"Luca," Ken said, his voice hardening, pushing his horror aside. "Call it in."

Luca's hands trembled as he pulled out his radio and relayed the message for a wagon to be dispatched. His voice was barely steady as he gave the address like it could crack at any moment. Just then, as if on cue, the police backup showed up with flashing lights and blaring sirens pulled up in front of Smalls' house, causing neighbors to peer through their windows and try to figure out what was going on.

Ken scanned the room again, taking in every detail. The open window, the blood-soaked sheets, and the gruesome arrangement of body parts. The image of the Hag, that twisted, wicked figure, loomed large in his mind, though he hadn't seen her himself. But he could sense her unmistakable presence, like a bad feeling that he just could not shake.

This wasn't just a crime scene. It was something primal and ancient. He didn't believe in the supernatural, but with everything Luca had explained to him, and standing in that room, surrounded by the aftermath of unspeakable violence, he felt the cold touch of death crawl up his spine.

He turned to face Smalls' father, who remained on his knees, gazing at the gruesome sight of his son's mangled body. The man's cries had subsided, leaving him in a state of shock and emptiness as he rocked back and forth.

The two detectives stood in silence, the room around them a gruesome reminder of the horror that continued to mark their city.

Both Luca and Ken knew they were out of their depth, that the lines between reality and nightmare had blurred in ways they couldn't yet understand. But they also knew they couldn't stop. This is who they were, and even at the cost of their own lives, they had to find the Hag quickly and stop her before more lives were destroyed.

CHAPTER 12

THE LAIR

The night hung over the Hag's hovel like a damp musty blanket, smothering the world outside. It was a night that seemed to swallow sound, sight, and even thought.

Officer Dobbs yanked yellow police tape across the row house's dilapidated entrance. The plastic strip disrupted the night with a sickly, artificial color, a stark contrast to the deep, consuming black that surrounded them. He'd done this a hundred times before, but tonight, something was different. He scanned the area, which seemed to pulse with hidden life as if the alley itself was alive.

Beside him, Officer Lloyd stood tense, his jaw clenched so tightly that the tendons in his neck stood out like cords. Lloyd was a fresh face on the force, but his presence carried a quiet confidence that hinted at the promise of a distinguished career ahead. Tall and athletic, with a build that spoke to his dedication to both his physical fitness and his commitment to the job, Lloyd moved with a purposeful stride that set him apart from the other rookies. His brown skin glistened under the moonlight, and his neatly cropped hair was always meticulously maintained, a small reflection of his disciplined nature.

Though he was still learning the ropes, there was an unmistakable sharpness in Lloyd's gaze—a keen awareness that absorbed everything happening around him. He had an instinct for the work, an ability to read situations and people with a perceptiveness that often took more seasoned officers by surprise.

Lloyd's uniform was always crisp, the creases in his shirt and pants sharp enough to cut, and his shoes polished to a mirror shine. His stint in the Marines taught him to take pride in the way he presented himself, understanding that first impressions mattered, especially in a profession where respect was earned, not given. There was a humility about him, too—an understanding that while he had promise, he still had much to learn. He listened more than he spoke, absorbing the wisdom of his superiors while quietly forming his own opinions.

Despite his relative inexperience, Lloyd had already shown flashes of brilliance on the job. He had a knack for de-escalating tense situations, his calm demeanor, and thoughtful approach often diffusing conflicts before they could spiral out of control. It was clear to anyone paying attention that Officer Lloyd was someone to watch—a young officer with the potential to rise quickly through the ranks if he continued on his current path.

But what truly set Lloyd apart was his unwavering sense of duty. He understood the weight of the badge he wore, the responsibility that came with it, and he carried that weight with a dignity that belied his years. There was a quiet strength in him, a drive to prove himself not just as a competent officer, but as someone who could make a real difference in the community he served.

Officer Brice approached from behind, her flashlight's beam jittering as she fought to keep her hands steady. Unlike Lloyd, she couldn't afford to show the slightest weakness, not in a place like this, not in a moment like this. The thin beam of light stabbed through the blackness but in an odd contained way. It was as if the beam could only cut so far into the dark. The edges were sharp, dropping off into nothingness.

Officer Brice was a study in contrasts, a woman who projected toughness but carried a quiet burden of self-doubt. Standing just a little over five feet tall, she was often underestimated at first glance, her petite frame seemingly at odds with the image of a hardened law enforcement officer. But what she lacked in stature, she made up for with a fierce persistence that radiated from her every move. In her early thirties, Brice was seasoned enough to know the ropes, but still young enough to feel the pressure of proving herself in a male-dominated world.

Brice's short-cropped hair, practical and no-nonsense, framed a face that was often set in a serious expression. Her brown eyes, sharp and observant, rarely missed a thing, yet there was an underlying tension there, a spark of uncertainty that she worked hard to mask. Her steadfastness was evident in everything she did, from the way she squared her shoulders when faced with a challenge to the firm set of her jaw when she was on the job.

Yet, for all her inner turmoil, Brice was respected by her peers. They saw her grit, her relentless work ethic, and the way she handled herself under pressure. She had earned her place in their ranks, even if she wasn't sure of it herself. And though the journey to self-assurance was still ongoing, there was no denying that Officer Brice had the courage of a fighter, one who would keep pushing forward, no matter the obstacles.

"Walsh said they'd be here soon," she murmured, her voice slicing through the silence like a blade, sharp and edged with anxiety.

Dobbs nodded, his gaze locked on the decrepit doorway of the house. "First perimeter sweep. Stay alert. No heroics. Call if you see anything."

Brice nodded back, her courage barely masking the anxiety seeping into her every movement. She moved off into the night, her light a fragile tether that barely held back the crushing intimidation of the unknown. Dobbs watched her go, his chest constricting with each step she took away from the relative safety of their small group.

Dobbs had a soft spot for Brice, one would say maybe even a crush on her. On one occasion he remembered approaching her desk, thinking he was being considerate by suggesting she sit out a rough call, only to be met with a steely resolve that he hadn't expected. She had clapped back with a firmness that left no room for misunderstanding—she didn't want special treatment, just the same respect as everyone else. Dobbs had walked away from that exchange with a new level of respect for Brice, realizing that she wasn't just another officer trying to prove herself; she was already every bit as capable as the rest of them, maybe even more so. The memory made him chuckle softly to himself—Brice was tough as nails, and he'd learned that lesson the hard way.

He turned to Lloyd, his voice dropping to an apprehensive tone. "Before Walsh gets here, we're gonna need to do another sweep inside, and by 'we' I mean you."

Lloyd recoiled, his face twisting with revulsion. "You kidding me? The smell in there... It's worse than death."

Dobbs' gaze was one of reluctant understanding. "Procedure is "procedure" for a reason. Get it done quick."

"Understood Sargent," Lloyd replied with respect despite his reluctance to do the sweep. He sure as hell didn't want to head into the Hag's hovel as it smelled bad enough on the outside, but he knew Dobbs was right. When you didn't follow "procedure," shit went wrong. His shoulders slumped in resignation as he flicked on his flashlight. The beam cut into the night as he ducked under the police tape and pushed open the rickety door. The creak of the hinges echoed in the night, a sound so mournful it could have come from the bowels of hell itself. The sound alone sent a shiver up Lloyd's spine. "Not a great way to start the evening," he thought.

As he stepped into the main room, the floorboards creaked underneath his feet, and the stench hit Lloyd hard, clawing at his senses with merciless ferocity. This wasn't just rot; it was something far more sinister, something that tore at the edges of sanity. Lloyd gagged almost immediately, covering his mouth and nose with his free arm, but it was futile. The smell seeped through, insinuating itself into his lungs, his bloodstream, his very soul. But he was going to do this, nothing would hold him back from proving he was worthy of the uniform.

The beam of his flashlight swept across the walls, revealing shelves cluttered with jars and twisted oddities. Each one was more grotesque than the last, leering at him, mocking his intrusion. His foot caught on a loose board, making him stumble and sending a jar of viscous yellow liquid crashing to the ground.

The glass shattered with a sharp crack, and an even more unbearable stench slammed into Lloyd, twisting his stomach and forcing him to gag. He'd faced down tense situations in his two years on the force, even at the wrong end of a gun, and never once doubted that police work was what he was meant for—but this was different. The foul odor invaded his senses, seeping into his skin, and his lungs, as if it were trying to suffocate him from the inside out. His pulse raced, panic clawing at the edges of his resolve. For the first time, a cold panic gripped him, making him wonder if he was cut out for this. No amount of bravery could shield him from the relentless, sickening stench that latched on to him like a parasite, threatening to unravel him completely.

"Goddammit!" he hissed, the sound reverberating off the walls, amplifying the grim mood that pressed in on him from all sides. Every nerve in his body screamed at him to get out, to run, but he was paralyzed by the sheer wrongness of the place.

"Lloyd, you okay in there?" Dobbs' voice crackled over the radio, the distortion barely concealing the worry in his tone.

Lloyd swallowed hard, his throat raw from the bile that threatened to rise again. "Yeah… fine," he lied, his voice barely more than a rasp. He forced his legs to move, dragging the beam of his flashlight across the walls. The light revealed strange symbols, markings etched in what could only be dried blood. They twisted and curled in unnatural patterns, speaking a secret language of pain and madness.

His stomach churned as the beam fell on something worse— severed heads, twisted and deformed, sitting on a shelf like trophies on display. Each one seemed frozen in a moment of agony, their hollow eye sockets staring back at him with silent screams.

Outside, Brice moved through the night like a ghost, her flashlight flicking up and down an alleyway. The beam revealed grimy concrete and bricks stained with God knows what, while the ground was littered with the refuse of a city that had long since stopped caring. The storm earlier that evening did little to wash away the stink of urban decay.

Her footsteps echoed in the confined space, each one a reminder of her isolation. Then, something moved at the far end of the alley—a quick, fleeting figure that vanished as soon as her light touched it. A shiver snaked down her spine, but as she swept her flashlight beam across the area, there was nothing. Just her mind playing tricks on her, she thought. The alley was empty, save for the rotting debris and her mounting fear.

Brice moved forward, checking every nook and cranny, including behind dumpsters, discarded furniture, and the occasional large kitchen appliance. Still nothing. Other than the sporadic breeze and movement of trash, the alley was quiet. Too quiet. Not a rat skittering about, or a stray cat searching through trash cans for a morsel. Hell, there wasn't even a cricket and for a moment she convinced herself she was the only living thing on the planet, and that everything else had disappeared leaving her to walk through purgatory alone. To make things worse, the shadows seemed to move in around her, thick and heavy. The darkness felt like a tangible force as if it could move and manipulate its surroundings with a will of its own.

And then, without warning, a voice whispered in her ear—soft, lilting, and filled with treachery. "Mary, Mary, quite contrary…"

A chill raced up her spine as she spun around, her flashlight penetrating the gloom, her nerves on edge. At the end of the alley, a figure loomed—a spectral form barely visible even by the intense flashlight beam. It was her, the Hag. A mass of rags and flesh twisted into a shape that defied nature.

She grabbed her walkie, her voice trembling as she spoke into it. "Dobbs?" She waited for a response, the seconds stretching into an eternity.

"Go for Dobbs," came the crackling reply.

But now she wasn't sure. The image seemed to dematerialize right in front of her as if the night swallowed the light of her flashlight beam. She swept the flashlight back and forth, but there was nothing. The alley was empty again. Her radio crackled indicating Dobbs was ready on the other end to check on her. She interrupted his callback and managed to squeak out, "Nothing... I'm heading back," she said, her voice a taut wire of unease.

"Copy that. Pick up some doughnuts on the way back," Dobbs' voice came through, trying for levity but failing. Brice allowed herself a thin smile, the tension easing just slightly.

"Jelly or powdered?" she asked, her tone lightening despite herself.

"Both," Dobbs replied, the connection still crackling with static.

She shook her head, the absurdity of their exchange was not lost on her. But as she turned back down the alley, something caught her eye—an unclear shape on the ground, one that hadn't been there before. Her heart leapt into her throat as she approached, the beam of her flashlight revealing the shape's true horror.

A human head, matted with blood, the eyes wide and staring, the mouth frozen in a scream of unimaginable terror. Brice's words caught in her throat, her body recoiling instinctively. "What the fuck?" she whispered, her voice barely audible over the throbbing in her ears.

Her hand went to her walkie, her fingers trembling as she pressed the button. "Dobbs?" she croaked, her voice laden with worry. She looked around for any sign of movement, but the night was still. Too still.

"Go for—" Dobbs' voice was cut off by a burst of static, the connection dimming out like a dying ember.

Brice's pulse pounded in her ears as she prodded the head with her boot, and it rolled over. Recognition hit her like a sledgehammer— it was Robert Smalls. The boy she had seen in the interrogation room earlier that day. The lifeless eyes of Robert Smalls stared back at her, his face twisted in that final, eternal scream of horror.

"Fuck!" she gasped, panic surging through her. She slammed her walkie again. "Goddammit, Dobbs, come in!"

Something behind her shifted, and Brice turned, her flashlight swinging wildly. A shape loomed behind her, and before she could react, the machete struck.

The blade bit deep into her neck, a searing pain that stole her voice. Blood spattered from the wound, showering the alley walls with crimson as she dropped to her knees. The Hag, her face a twisted mask of evil, wrenched the machete free with a sickening crunch.

Brice's vision blurred, the world spinning as she struggled to breathe. She could taste the acrid taste of blood as it filled her mouth and made her choke on her pleas for help. She reached for her weapon, but her fingers were clumsy and unresponsive. The darkness closed in, wrapping her in an unwelcome embrace.

THWACK! The machete came down again, splitting her neck halfway. Brice's body convulsed, her eyes rolling back into her head as the blade held her upright in death's cruel grip.

CHAPTER 13

WHISPERS IN THE DARK

Dobbs paced in front of the hovel, he scanned the perimeter nervously. He listened intently for any sound, any sign that Brice was coming back. His fingers tightened around the radio as he spoke into it again, his voice laced with concern. "Brice? Come on, Brice, talk to me."

The only response was the soft crackle of static. His stomach churned with a growing sense of impending doom. He had sent her out there, and now… nothing.

Dobbs pacing became more and more frantic "Brice should have been back by now," he thought.

Out of nowhere, the silence was broken by a loud sound that echoed behind him. Dobbs quickly turned, his hand automatically reaching for his holstered weapon. But it was only Lloyd, bursting out of the front door with a face as white as a sheet. He stumbled forward, heaving for air, his body bent over as if someone had just landed a blow straight to his gut.

Lloyd's shoulders convulsed as he retched violently, the sound echoing through the still night, only amplifying the sense of wrongness that engulfed him in a poisonous fog.

"Lloyd?" Dobbs called out, his voice edged with concern. He moved closer but kept a wary distance. Lloyd had been inside for too long, exposed to whatever horrors that place held.

After he caught his breath, Lloyd wiped his mouth with a shaking hand as if he were struggling to shake off a nightmare that wouldn't let go.

"I— I'm okay," Lloyd began, but his voice cracked, and he doubled over again, dry heaving, his body shuddering violently. "Fuck…"

Dobbs' grip on his walkie tightened. He turned away from Lloyd, facing the lair's entrance, and tried once more to reach Brice. "Come on, Brice. Just get back here, alright?"

But the response was the same—only static.

The distant rumble of a car engine grew louder as it approached the alley. Dobbs turned to face the source of the noise, watching as the headlights illuminated the area. The car came to a stop and two figures emerged from inside. Although only their silhouettes were visible, Dobbs could recognize the two detectives by the way they carried themselves. Their flashlights flicked on, sending beams of light slicing through the gloom. The light caught Dobbs' face, and he squinted against it, raising a hand to shield his eyes.

"Dobbs," Ken called, his voice steady and assertive as he approached.

"Detectives," Dobbs replied, trying to steady his voice, but the anxiety in his tone was unmistakable.

"What's with him?" Luca asked, pointing to Lloyd, who was holding himself up against the side of the row house, still heaving as if his body were trying to expel some deep-rooted poison.

"I had him clear the place before you got here," Dobbs explained. "The smell… It's pretty unbearable, sir." He looked toward the building as if it might reveal its secrets at any moment.

Luca snapped on a pair of latex gloves and handed another set to Ken. "No electricity in there either?" Luca asked, his voice low, almost as if he didn't want the night to hear.

Dobbs shook his head. "No, sir. The whole place is dead." Luca nodded in acknowledgment, as he stepped past him.

The door creaked open as Luca pushed it with his flashlight. The beam traced the interior walls, revealing twisted imagery strange symbols, grotesque artifacts, and shelves lined with jars that seemed to pulse with a sickly, internal glow.

Ken and Luca stepped inside, the smell hitting them immediately—a rancid blend of rot and decay, almost palpable in its intensity that seemed to seep into their very pores.

"Christ, it smells like something died in here," Ken muttered, as he pulled a handkerchief from his pocket and covered his mouth and nose. "What the hell is it?" His voice was muffled, but the disgust was clear.

"Everything," Luca responded, his voice also muffled by the makeshift mask he pieced together from his handkerchief. He fastened it behind his head and covered his nose and mouth, attempting to shield himself from the overpowering stench. With a flick of his flashlight, he scanned the room, freezing as the beam illuminated an unexpected object: a tarnished crown resting on top of a pile of yellowed papers atop a makeshift desk. "What in the world?" Luca muttered, cautiously approaching the crown while crunching debris underfoot with each step.

"What is it?" Ken asked, immediately curious.

"I'm not sure," Luca admitted as he picked up the tarnished crown. It was surprisingly heavier than he imagined. It felt solid, smooth, and well-crafted. "It can't be," he thought as he rubbed his thumb along it removing the slight tarnish that made it seem nothing more than a rusty hunk of metal. But clear as day, underneath that thin layer of grime shone gold. "Jesus," Luca let slip.

At that moment, Ken's flashlight swept across the walls, illuminating satanic symbols etched in what appeared to be dried blood. In the center of the wall, an inverted pentagram was painted to encircle the depiction of two seated figures holding a sword and a scepter, their gaze seeming to follow the intruders with malicious intent. "Stop…there," Luca urged.

"Do you recognize any of this?" Ken asked, his voice low, as if speaking too loudly might awaken something.

Luca nodded reluctantly, his fingers tracing the air just above the figures, careful not to touch the wall itself. "Sort of… It looks like a royal seal inside a pentagram," he said, his voice tinged with apprehension. "It's her," he declared while holding up the crown for Ken to see.

"Look at this," Luca added indicating the crown.

Ken's gaze immediately gravitated toward the glimmering spot of gold amidst tarnish. "Is that… real? He asked incredulously. Luca confirmed his suspicion with a simple nod before placing the crown back where he found it. "How is that even possible?"

"I stopped asking those questions fifteen years ago," Luca replied, as he reached for a worn and tattered book that caught his eye on the dusty shelves. He put down his flashlight and turned to Ken. "Could you shine some light on this?"

Ken held the light while Luca opened the book and began scanning its pages. The faded scribbles, cryptic symbols, and incomplete words were etched onto the surface, their meaning shrouded in layers of time and dirt.

Luca's fingers gently turned to another sheet, one that felt different, more ominous. The paper was stiff, brittle, and stained with something recognizable—something that had once been alive. Scratched into the surface, in what he now realized was dried blood, was a single name.

"LEGIO."

The name caught him off guard and his face went pale. The weight of it hit him hard, sinking into his gut like a heavy stone. This was the worst possible outcome he could have imagined.

Ken noticed something was wrong with Luca right away. "Hey, are you okay?" he asked, concerned. Luca shook his head slowly. "No."

Turning to face Ken, Luca held up the blood-stained paper for him to see. His voice was barely above a whisper as he spoke. "This... Demon. She's making sacrifices to him."

Luca's face remained transfixed as he stared at the name etched onto the paper. The recognition was immediate, and the horror was palpable. "The demon," he confirmed, fighting with all his might to suppress the terror it provoked inside of him. Luca shook his head. "It's the same one the little girl had. The one I told you about."

Ken's mind spun with restlessness and confusion, desperately trying to grasp the implications of Luca's words. "One demon, but endless forms," Luca spoke with a chilling calmness, but underneath there was a blazing urgency. "It can manipulate your perception, show you what it wants you to see." With a sinking feeling in his gut, Ken realized the true danger of facing this shape-shifting demon.

Ken sighed, and ran a hand through his hair, his bravado failing to hide the concern beneath. "Then how... How did you get rid of it?"

Luca's response was immediate, his voice laced with an edge of hopelessness. "We didn't."

Ken felt a shiver run down his spine. "There's something you can do, right? You saved the little girl, didn't you?"

Luca shook his head. "She didn't make it." His gaze was distant, haunted by memories he wished he could forget. "We figured it out too late. The Gospel of Mark tells the story of where Christ made a deal with this "Legion," instead of sending him back to hell, he allowed the demons to occupy a herd of nearby grazing pigs. The entire herd—about two thousand pigs—rushed down a steep bank into the Sea of Galilee and drowned."

Ken's gut instinct, sharpened from years of dealing with the darkest of human behavior, urged him to brush it off as mere superstition. But the intensity in Luca's gaze and the weight of his words made it impossible to ignore. Everything seemed to fall into place perfectly. This was the missing link, one that couldn't be denied. The nursery rhyme, Mary Tudor, and the cryptic message in Aramaic all fit together in a narrative he didn't want to believe. As much as he tried to find a logical explanation, everything pointed towards an unsettling truth.

Luca could see the turmoil in Ken's mind and wished he could make it easier for him to understand, but deep down he knew that some things were beyond rationalization.

Outside the stillness of the night was disturbing. Lloyd wiped the vomit from his mouth with a crumpled piece of paper from his notepad, his face pale, his skin clammy with sweat. His hands trembled slightly, betraying the fear that had settled deep in his bones. "Where the hell is Brice?" Dobbs muttered more to himself than anyone else, his voice edged with unease, his brow furrowed with worry. "In two minutes we're going to search," he added.

The crackle of Dobbs' shoulder radio disturbed the heavy silence, startling Lloyd and filling him with hope. He fumbled for the button, his fingers slipping before finally pressing it down. "Brice?" Dobbs said into the device, his voice tense, filled with an anticipation that made the hairs on the back of Lloyd's neck stand on end.

For a moment, there was nothing but static, and then—faint but unmistakable—a discordant voice sang back, soft and haunting, "Mary, Mary, quite contrary…"

As the words hit Dobbs' ears, a chill spread through his body like icy fingers gripping his spine. He exchanged a wide-eyed look with Lloyd, both men momentarily frozen by the eerie, childlike sing-song that floated through the speaker of the radio.

"What the hell?" Lloyd shouted, his voice cracking with worry, scanning the area as if the walls of the alleyway were whispering the nursery rhyme.

Dobbs didn't hesitate. Years of training kicked in, pushing down the apprehension that bit at his insides. His hand flew to his holster, drawing his revolver with practiced ease, the weight of the weapon grounding him in the midst of the rising panic.

Lloyd mirrored his actions, pulling out his gun, and the two officers moved in unison as they circled the block of attached row houses and down the myriad of crooked alleys. Their footsteps were quick and intentional, each step a reminder that Brice was alone out there without backup. The stress was enough to choke on. They knew, without a doubt, that something was out there, waiting for them.

The two officers moved cautiously down one narrow damp alleyway to another and then another. It was a maze of back alleys jammed behind the cacophony of row houses that had been built haphazardly at the end of the Second World War in support of nearby factories now long gone. Their flashlight beams were little comfort in the never-ending blackness. Every nerve in their bodies was on edge, their senses heightened, attuned to every rustle, every hint of movement.

"Brice?" Dobbs called out, his voice bouncing off the grimy, graffiti-streaked walls, only to be swallowed by the encroaching blackness.

A scurrying noise from overhead stopped them both in their tracks. Their bodies stiffened, their flashlights jolting up towards the rooftops that loomed on either side of the narrow alley. Their fear intensified and spread like wildfire through their veins. The beams of light caught fleeting glimpses of something moving just beyond the edge of their vision.

"Mary, Mary…" The Hag's voice whispered again, this time so close it felt as though it was right in Dobbs' ear. He spun around, his gun raised, expecting to find someone standing behind him. But there was nobody.

"You hear that?" Dobbs asked, his voice betraying the unease he tried to suppress.

"What… no," Lloyd replied, his voice barely a whisper, his senses were on alert, as he scanned the alley from side to side. The fear was contagious, spreading between them like wildfire.

They pressed onward, the beams of their flashlights sweeping across the dingy alley walls, illuminating only more graffiti, mounds of garbage, and the musty stench of decay. However, the feeling of being watched was unshakeable, as though something was lurking just beyond their vision. A tingling sensation slithered up their backs and made their skin crawl. It was as if they were being hunted by a creature that could hide in front of their very eyes.

"I don't like this… Call for backup," Dobbs ordered, his voice low, almost lost in the silence that seemed to swallow every sound.

Lloyd nodded, his hand going to the radio clipped to his shoulder. "Lloyd to Dispatch. Come in," he said, his voice steady despite the tension overtaking him.

The response was only static, a harsh reminder of how alone they were.

"Dispatch?" Lloyd repeated, his voice rising in pitch, a note of anxiety creeping in as the static continued. "Detective Walsh? Anyone?"

"Quite contrary…" The Hag's voice hissed directly into Lloyd's ear, so close he could feel the warmth of the words on his skin. He whipped around, his flashlight beam slashing through the darkness, his gun following suit. But there was nothing—only shadows, deeper and blacker than before, engulfing them from all sides.

"What is it, did you hear it?" Dobbs asked

"Yes. Who's that?" Lloyd shouted, his voice raw with tension, his flashlight beam shaking as it forced its way through the murky night, desperate to find the source of the voice. "Something right in my ear."

At the end of the alleyway, a body tumbled out from behind a corner, landing with a sickening thud on the wet pavement. The sound echoed in the narrow confines of the alley.

"Jesus. Brice?" Dobbs called out, his flashlight snapping to the figure on the ground, his heart sinking at the sight.

The body stirred slightly, a faint sign of life amidst the otherwise lifeless alley. "She's alive!" Lloyd shouted, a surge of hope in his voice as he rushed forward, his flashlight beam bobbing wildly.

"Wait!" Dobbs called after him, but Lloyd was already crouched next to Brice's body, his relief turning to horror as he realized what he was seeing.

Brice's head was missing. Blood pooled around the jagged stump of her neck, the flashlight beam caught the glistening edges of the wound. The red gleam of it reflected back like a macabre beacon of death. Lloyd stumbled back, his stomach fluids once more rising in his throat as the reality of it hit him.

"We need to leave!" Dobbs shouted, his voice carrying down the alley, but it was too late.

From behind the corner, Brice's head rolled out, stopping at Lloyd's feet with a grotesque finality. Her lifeless gaze stared up at him, wide and frozen in a final, silent cry of terror. Lloyd screamed, a sound filled with raw horror. All his training left him and instinct took over and he turned to flee.

The Hag emerged from the dark as if she hadn't stepped out from it so much as materialized from nothing, her machete raised high, her eyes gleaming with twisted delight. THWACK! The blade split Lloyd's head down the middle with a gruesome crack that echoed in the narrow alley, the sound of shattering bone filling the air with a sickening finality. Blood and brain matter splattered against the ground.

"Lloyd!!" Dobbs yelled, his gun aimed and firing repeatedly, the sudden bursts of light illuminating the alley. The bullets ripped into the Hag's chest as she let out a deep, gurgling laugh. Black blood dribbled from her mouth as she dropped to her knees and collapsed onto the ground with a heavy thump.

"Fuck!" Dobbs yelled as he ran up to the bodies, his hands shaking with adrenaline and fear.

CHAPTER 14

INTO THE ABYSS

As they continued to search the room, something glinted just at the edge of Ken's flashlight beam. Ken adjusted his beam to bring it into the light. "Luca…" he croaked as he realized what he was looking at. The light was the eye-shine of Mason's lone eyeball reflecting at them.

"No, God no," Luca gasped.

BAM! BAM! BAM!

Gunshots broke the trance of the two detectives. Luca and Ken instinctively flicked their flashlights towards the entrance. "Dobbs!" Ken exclaimed, both men turning and making a beeline for the door.

They burst out of the Hag's place, the door slamming behind them with a sharp crack that echoed through the night. For a moment, they stood still, chests heaving, eyes darting, the air like a slap to the face after the suffocating gloom inside. The world outside felt disorienting, they spun in place, trying to get their bearings. Every direction felt wrong until another shot echoed through the night, sending the group into a frenzy.

"This way!" Ken shouted, leading the charge as they sprinted towards an alleyway. They dashed down its long stretch and took a sharp turn at the end, following the sound of gunfire in the distance. As they turned another corner, Dobbs came into view, standing under the light of the moon with his gun pointed forward. Smoke drifted from the barrel as he pulled the trigger repeatedly, but no bullets were left to fire.

At his feet lay the Hag, her icy grip still wrapped around Dobbs' ankle. "Dobbs, move!" Luca screamed as he ran towards his friend. Dobbs stumbled back as the Hag's hand released him, his body trembling uncontrollably. He stared into nothingness, unseeing and lost. Ken rushed over and grabbed the gun from Dobbs' quivering hand, trying to bring him out of his trance. "Come on, Dobbs, talk to me!"

Luca pulled out his radio. "Marchetti to Dispatch," he called, his voice strained with urgency as he glanced around the alley. The response was static, cold, and empty, offering no comfort, and no connection to the outside world. "God damn it, Dispatch, come in!" He yelled.

Ken guided Dobbs toward the wall, easing him down to the ground. "Sit for a minute," he said, his voice soft, trying to ground Dobbs in the present, in reality. Dobbs sat there, his mind distant, staring into the abyss.

"Dispatch!?" Luca repeated into the radio, but again, only static greeted him. Luca focused on the prostrate body of the Hag. A sudden realization came flooding to him. "Ken! Move away from him."

Ken looked at Luca, confused. "We need to get him out of here!"

"Please, just move away from him," Luca insisted, his voice tinged with urgency that Ken couldn't ignore. He pointed to the body. "Look."

Ken took a few steps back as he noticed the Hag's body on the ground. But it wasn't the Hag anymore. Grimes lay dead in her place, her face twisted in an expression of pure terror. "Grimes?" Ken whispered, his voice barely audible as the realization hit him.

A scraping sound drew their attention. The machete, now stained with fresh blood, moved ever so slightly, dragging itself across the ground as if possessed by an untenable force. The blade glinted ominously in the moonlight as it moved, sending a shiver down Ken's spine.

"What the hell?" Ken's voice trembled, barely above a whisper, as they both stared at the impossible sight unfolding before them. The machete moved with a purpose, sliding through the trash and debris toward Dobbs. Ken and Luca watched in stunned silence as it disappeared into the shadows where Dobbs sat slumped against the wall. "Dobbs?" Ken called out, his voice echoing through the narrow alley. There was no response, only the unnatural quiet that seemed to amplify the terror rushing through their veins.

Out of nowhere, a low, cackling laugh echoed through the alley, a sound filled with sinister, twisted joy. Dobb's voice, but different now—distorted, unnatural.

"Dobbs?!" Luca shouted, his voice tinged with desperation as he moved closer, his flashlight beam leading the way.

Ken strained to see, but all he could make out was a murky figure where Dobbs had been sitting. The figure shifted, slowly rising to its feet, and as it stepped into the light, their worst fears were confirmed.

The Hag had returned. She stepped into the beam of Ken's flashlight, her form hunched and grotesque, brandishing the machete. Her mouth twisted into that sickening grin as she watched the two men with an unsettling intensity.

"Christ," Ken muttered softly. He raised his gun, his hands shaking, but Luca grabbed his arm, stopping him.

"Dobbs!"

"He's not Dobbs!" Ken snapped, his voice filled with frustration and panic. Luca couldn't believe what he was seeing, but there was something else there—a glimmer of recognition, of terrible understanding.

"Dobbs… he's in there. Maybe…" Luca's voice wavered as he stared at the Hag, his mind racing to make sense of the impossible.

The Hag cocked her head to one side, and stared at them with a twisted delight as she sang, "How does your garden grow?" Her voice was a haunting lullaby, the words dripping with malice and perverse amusement.

Ken's finger trembled on the trigger as he aimed the gun at her, but the uncertainty in Luca's eyes made him hesitate. "Is Dobbs in there?" Ken demanded, his voice rising with urgency, desperate for an answer.

Luca could only shake his head in doubt as all of the color drained from his face. "Yes, Dobbs is in there somewhere!"

The Hag's grin widened, her mouth stretching impossibly wide as she let out a deep, feral scream that sent a wave of fear straight through Ken and Luca. The sound blast through the alley, shaking the very walls, and consuming any sound in its path.

In a flash, the Hag pounced, her movements inhumanly fast as she came down on top of Ken, knocking him to the ground. His gun flew from his hand, sliding across the pavement as she crouched over him, her weight pressing down, her hot and rancid breath against his face.

Luca raised his weapon, aiming point-blank at the Hag, his hands trembling. But before he could pull the trigger, the Hag leaned in closer to Ken, her lips inches from his face, glistening with that deadly spittle. "With silver bells and cockle shells..." she crooned, her voice a mockery of a nursery rhyme, each word dripping with venom.

Ken could see the deadly saliva threatening to drop on his face with every move she made. "Don't! If any of that shit falls on me, I'm done," he warned his voice tight with anxiety and desperation.

The Hag grinned eerily, her head tilting back and forth as she continued her twisted serenade. "And pretty maids all in a row..." Her arm cocked back, the machete gleaming in the moonlight as she prepared to strike.

"Mary Tudor?!" Luca blurted out, desperate to distract her. The Hag froze, her head snapping toward Luca with a look of curious confusion. Her eyes narrowed as if trying to place where she had heard that name before. Luca seized the moment, signaling for Ken to move. "Only surviving child of Catherine of Aragon," Luca continued his voice shaky, "Daughter of Henry the Eighth. I'm running out of history here!" He shouted to Ken, the desperation clear in his tone.

The Hag's mouth opened wider and cracked at the joints as if the sinew and muscles that kept her jaw in place were ripping apart. Again she let out that horrific deep, guttural scream. The sound shook their bones, the noise almost tangible in intensity.

But the distraction was all Ken needed. With a surge of adrenaline, he shoved the Hag to one side, just as Luca unloaded his weapon into her. "Bam! Bam! Bam!" Each shot drove the Hag back, her body convulsing violently with every impact.

"Ken!" Luca shouted, his voice filled with a mix of frustration and alarm. The Hag lay bullet-ridden on the ground, her body twitching among the trash and debris. Luca rushed to Ken's side, his mind on high alert as he helped his partner to his feet. "Did she get anything on you?" Luca asked, his voice shaking with concern.

"No, I'm okay." Ken's voice was shaky, but he managed to pull himself together, reaching down to grab his weapon.

As Ken's fingers brushed the cold metal of his gun, the Hag's body sprang to life. With a speed that defied belief, her arm stretched to three times its length, grabbing Ken's wrist with an iron grip, her nails digging into his flesh. The pain shot up his arm like wildfire, and he fought to break free, but her hold was unyielding, her strength inhuman.

"No!" Luca's voice tore through the night, raw and desperate, as he lunged at the Hag. He grabbed for her grotesquely elongated hand, his fingers curling around the cold, unnatural flesh, trying to pry it away from Ken. The struggle was fierce, a chaotic blur of movement in the dim alley, where every shadow seemed to twist and writhe with malice.

Ken staggered, his balance lost in the fray. He tumbled backward, colliding with a pair of rusted trash cans. The metallic clatter echoed through the narrow alley as the cans toppled over, sending a cascade of refuse spilling onto the wet pavement. Ken hit the ground hard, the impact jarring, the air knocked from his lungs as he struggled to regain his footing, the weight of the night's horrors pressing down on him.

The Hag's grip shifted, her arms and legs wrapped around Luca like a vise. He struggled to break free, his body twitching and shaking as the Hag tightened her hold, her nails digging deeper into his skin. Luca's face contorted in pain, he was filled with terror as he felt the life being drained from him.

Ken scrambled on his belly, dazed but determined, his vision blurred but he forced himself to focus. He managed to grab his gun, his hands shaking as he tried to line up a shot. Finally, the Hag fell silent, her arms and legs went limp as she released Luca. He collapsed to the ground, shaking and looking into the emptiness, his stare vacant, his body trembling uncontrollably.

"Marchetti?!" Ken called out desperately, his voice echoing through the alley, but there was no answer. Ken pushed himself to his feet. "Talk to me, Luca!" he pleaded, but Luca remained silent, staring blankly ahead.

"Mary… Mary…" Luca said, his voice barely audible, filled with a strange, detached calm that sent chills down Ken's spine. Tears streamed down Ken's face as he aimed the gun at his friend, his hands trembling. "Please, don't make me do this!" he cried, his voice breaking as he struggled with the weight of the decision before him. It felt like a twisted echo of an old story, one where the hero had to make an impossible choice, like a boy forced to put down his best friend in Old Yeller.

Luca fought for control, his voice wavering as he begged, "Shoot me… please." But then his voice changed, taking on a sinister tone as he continued," Quite contrary…"

"No!" Ken backed away, his aim faltering. "Shoot…" Luca's voice faded as he collapsed to the ground, his body jerking and convulsing as if possessed by some demonic force. And then, all at once, he fell silent.

As Luca lay there, in the alleyway where the world seemed to fold in on itself, he felt something deep within him stir, like a beast waking from a long, restless sleep. The air was thick with the scent of decay and damp concrete, mingling with the coppery tang of blood still fresh on his hands. His lungs felt heavy, weighted down by an invisible force that was tightening around his chest, squeezing the life out of him, one breath at a time.

A low hum started in his ears, like the drone of a thousand locusts, growing louder until it was a shrieking cacophony that rattled his brain. He pressed his hands against his head as if trying to keep it from splitting open, but it was no use. His fingers clawed at his scalp, desperate, but they couldn't stop the pressure building inside him. Luca's vision blurred, the edges of the world smearing into black, oily shadows that danced and writhed like living things. His heart was a wild drumbeat in his chest, hammering out a frantic rhythm as if trying to match the madness surging through his veins. He could feel it now, something crawling under his skin, something that wasn't him—something that had been waiting, biding its time, until this very moment.

And then, with a sudden, sickening jolt, Luca's body jerked, as though it had been seized by an electric current. His bones felt like they were being twisted and reshaped, pulled apart by unseen hands. The pain was immediate and all-consuming, a searing agony that ripped through his muscles, his tendons, his very marrow. He opened his mouth to scream, but the sound that emerged was not his own. It was a guttural, animalistic howl, something primal and terrifying, a sound that didn't belong in this world. His skin stretched and bubbled, flesh warping as his bones shifted beneath it, reshaping, reforming.

His fingers elongated, nails blackening into sharp, jagged claws that tore at the air.

His face, once familiar, now contorted into something grotesque—a twisted mask of terror and hatred, mouth stretching far wider than any human mouth should ever go. He could feel his teeth growing, sharpening into jagged points that scraped against each other like rusty blades. Inside his head, Luca's thoughts were a jumbled mess, fragments of memory and consciousness colliding and shattering into a thousand pieces. He could feel the Hag's presence, an ancient and malevolent force, slithering through his mind like a snake, coiling itself around every thought, every fear, every desperate hope. It called to him, in a voice that was both his and not his, a voice that hissed and snarled and dripped with venom.

Ken watched in horror as Luca's body began to change, shifting and contorting in ways that no human body should. It was as if something inside him was forcing its way out, twisting his flesh into a new, grotesque form.

"Let go," the voice inside Luca spoke, its words like ice-cold fingers sliding down his spine. "Let go and let me in. This is what you were meant for. This is what you've always been." Luca tried to fight it, tried to hold on to the last remnants of his sanity, but it was a futile battle. The Hag was too strong, Legion was too strong, too ancient, too deeply rooted in the evil that had always lingered just beneath the surface. He could feel himself slipping away, his thoughts unraveling until all that was left was a cold, hollow emptiness.

And then, with a final, agonizing twist, Luca was gone. The Hag was firmly in his place, a twisted grin spreading across her face. She raised her talon like hands, admiring the work she had done, feeling the power thrumming through her new form, a power that had been denied to her for far too long.

The Hag sprung to her feet and turned her gaze toward Ken, her lips curling into that smile that was nothing short of monstrous. She was once again free now, free to do as she pleased, to wreak havoc and terror on those who had dared to cross her path. And as she took her first step forward, the ground beneath her seemed to tremble, as if the very earth itself knew what was coming and recoiled in horror.

She stared at Ken, her mouth stretching into a grin that was far too wide, far too human to belong to something so monstrous. "Vindictam exigo!" the Hag shrieked, her voice echoing through the alley like a curse.

Ken didn't wait to see what would happen next. He turned and ran, his mind racing with panic and confusion, the Hag's scream followed him through the alley. He knew he had to find a way to end this nightmare, a way to save his friend, but the horror of what he had just witnessed left him questioning whether there was any hope at all. His breath came in irregular gasps, his chest pounding fiercely as he raced through the labyrinth of death and despair. The alley seemed to stretch endlessly before him, a twisted maze of disquiet from which there was no escape.

As he skidded around a corner, he saw a shimmer of light in the distance. Hope surged through him like a beacon in the night. It was his car, parked at the edge of the alley, a symbol of salvation amidst the chaos. With renewed zeal, Ken pushed himself to run faster, ignoring the burning ache in his muscles and focusing only on reaching safety. The alley seems to taunt him, elongating with each step he took, as if testing his resolve. But Ken refused to back down. He knew that his only chance lay in reaching that familiar metal frame that held the promise of freedom. His mind drowned out the eerie whispers that threatened to cloud his thoughts, steeling his resolve as he sprinted towards his car.

Finally, after what felt like an eternity of running through a nightmare made real, Ken's outstretched hand brushed against the cold metal of his car door. With a surge of relief, he yanked it open and plunged inside slamming the car door behind him, the solid thud echoing through the empty alley. The click of the lock followed a sound of finality in the silence. The engine roared as he mashed down on the gas. His hands gripped the steering wheel, but it was more out of a need to steady himself than to control the car. The dashboard lights blinked wearily, casting a dim glow that felt more like a haunting than a guide. Ken's eyes, once sharp and vigilant, were now dulled by fatigue, and confusion, were shifting anxiously to the rearview mirror, half-expecting to see something—anything—lurking in the shadows behind him.

When he shifted into gear, the leapt forward. His knuckles tightened on the wheel out of a desperate attempt to keep going, to push through the haze of exhaustion that was clouding his mind. The night air seeped in through the cracked window, cold and unforgiving, chilling him to the bone. It felt like a phantom's icy hand on the back of his neck, a reminder that he was not alone, that something unseen was watching, waiting for him to falter. Every creak of the car's metal, every distant sound, echoes in his mind like a sinister lullaby, lulling him closer to the edge of collapse.

He pushed on, but it was a losing battle. A mile dragged by, each second ticking away with agonizing slowness. The muted hum of the engine blended with the sound of his labored, uneven breaths, a chorus of weariness that weighed him down with every passing moment. Finally, it became too much. The fatigue of having been on constant alert crashed down on him at once. With a shaky hand, he pulled the car to the side of the road, the screech of brakes cutting through the oppressive silence like a cry for help. The engine sputtered and died, and Ken slumped back in his seat. He was done—at least for now.

The road ahead would have to wait; he needed a second, just one, to gather what was left of his strength before he could even think about moving forward again. He sat there for a moment, gripping the steering wheel tightly, trying to steady himself, trying to make sense of the chaos that had just unfolded. His mind was a storm, swirling with images and thoughts that refused to settle. "How do you even begin to fight something like that?" He asked himself, the question one he feared he could never answer. It felt like a nightmare, one he couldn't wake from, trapped in a world where the rules of reality no longer applied.

Ken looked around the pitch-black streets outside his vehicle. The shadows seemed to shift and move, playing tricks on his mind, making him question what was real and what was just a figment of his terror. Every glimmer of light, every rustle of leaves sent a jolt of adrenaline through him, as if at any moment the nightmare would come crashing down on him again.

He reached for the radio handset, his fingers trembling slightly as he pressed the mic button. His voice, though steady, carried the weight of everything he had seen. "Walsh to dispatch," he said, his tone urgent, the voice of a man who had looked into the abyss and wasn't sure he'd make it back.

"Go for dispatch," came the crackling response, a small lifeline in the chaos.

"Code 999, I repeat 999. Send a wagon and backup, to the last address. The suspect is armed and on foot. Do not engage. I repeat, do not engage! Get them in and out as fast as possible. Copy?" Ken's voice was firm, leaving no room for misunderstanding. This was a situation unlike any other, and he knew better than to let anyone else get caught in the crossfire.

"Roger that, Detective," the reply came, calm and professional, a stark contrast to the confusion Ken had just escaped. He returned the mic to its cradle with a deliberate motion, as if trying to cling to the last threads of control he had. For a brief moment, it looked like he might lose it—the sheer weight of the night's horrors threatening to crack his composure. But then, with a deep, resolute exhale, he braced himself. His gaze hardened, the steel returning to him as he turned the key in the ignition. The engine roared to life, and Ken pulled away from the side of the road, the night swallowing him whole.

CHAPTER 15

THE BAIT

He had been up for nearly twenty-four hours, but sleep was the last thing on his mind. The morning light was just beginning to filter through the small window in Luca's kitchen, bouncing off the spotless countertops. Ken moved through the small apartment with the weariness of a man who had seen too much, his body heavy with exhaustion, his mind still racing. His eyes were bloodshot, his face unshaven, a ghost of the man who had started the day before. "There's something here," he muttered to himself, his voice barely above a whisper, "I know it."

He rubbed a hand over his face, trying to wipe away the memories that clung to him like cobwebs. He had to focus on the task at hand and couldn't be drawn down by what had just happened. He reached for the Italian mocha pot on the counter, fumbling with it in his fatigue. The metallic clink of the pot against the counter echoed through the quiet room.

"Dammit," he muttered, shoving the pot aside in frustration. He'd seen Luca make coffee in this Rubik's cube of a coffee maker a hundred times, but still couldn't figure it out. It clattered against a stack of books, threatening to topple them before settling back into place. The sound reverberated through the stillness, a harsh reminder of his helplessness.

But then, as the noise faded, something caught his eye—a book, its worn leather cover standing out among the rest. It was Luca's Bible. His gaze locked onto it, a spark of determination igniting in his weary mind. He grabbed it, flipping through the pages with a feverish intensity.

"Where did he say it was?" Ken muttered to himself, his fingers rifling through the thin pages, the sound of paper rustling filling the room. "Come on, come on…"

Ken's finger traced the ancient lines of text, the delicate pages of the Bible rustling under his touch. The light filtering through the small kitchen window seemed to sharpen, throwing long shadows that danced across the countertop. He sank into a kitchen chair and locked on the words as if they held the very essence of life itself. "The Gospel according to Mark." His pulse quickened, thumping in his ears, drowning out everything else as he read.

The world outside faded into a distant hum, leaving the silent intensity of the text before him. Each word etched itself into his mind, burning with an urgency that coursed through his veins, igniting something deep within him that he hadn't known existed.

As he reached the passage, a shiver ran down his spine, his hands gripping the fragile pages as if they were his only tether to reality. The text seemed to pulse with hidden power, the words blurring and sharpening in his vision, almost as if they were alive.

A low gasp escaped his lips as the truth unfurled itself before him—not in a gentle whisper, but in a thunderous roar that shook him to his core.

He snapped the Bible shut with a resounding clap, the sound ricocheting off the walls, reverberating through the stillness of the kitchen. Ken sat frozen for a moment, the silence that followed filled with a palpable tension, as though the very air around him was immobile. His gaze remained fixed on the closed book, his reflection in the polished surface of the table staring back at him—eyes wide, unblinking, alive with a fierce, newfound clarity.

His hand moved instinctively to the cell phone in his pocket his fingers hovered over the screen, and then, with sudden decisiveness, he began to dial, his hand steady, the plan crystallizing in his mind with each tap.

The quiet resolve in his movements spoke volumes, the transformation within him so profound it seemed to radiate outward, filling the small kitchen with a sense of purpose that was almost tangible. Ken was no longer the man who had stumbled into this nightmare; he had become something else—something relentless, something driven by the truth that had seared itself into his very soul. At that moment, it felt as though the entire world had shifted, tilted on its axis, poised on the brink of something monumental. Ken was brimming with an intensity that hadn't been there before. He was ready, and he knew what he needed to do.

The line rang, each tone echoing in the quiet apartment until a voice answered on the other end.

"Laura, it's Ken. I need that favor," he said, his tone urgent yet composed, the voice of a man who had just seen too much to explain over the phone.

There was a brief pause before Laura Weston replied, her voice filled with concern. "What's going on?" she asked, her words laced with worry, but also trust.

"I'll explain on the way. Just get here fast, I also need you to pick up some things for me, I'll text it to you," Ken responded, already moving with purpose to gather his things. "And coffee please, black," he begged as he grabbed his coat, slipping it on with a sense of perseverance that belied his weariness.

It wasn't long after Ken sent the text that he could hear the sound of Laura's car pulling up outside Luca's apartment. Her horn beeped twice quickly in succession letting Ken know she had arrived. He zipped down a flight of stairs and stepped out into the morning air, the short overnight respite from the heat was already gone, and it promised to be another sweltering day. Laura sat behind the wheel, her expression a mix of curiosity and concern as she took in Ken's disheveled appearance.

"Get in," she said simply, searching his face for answers that he wasn't ready to give just yet. Ken slid into the passenger seat, the faint scent of her perfume a small comfort in the midst of the chaos.

"I need Vito Matthews," Ken told Laura with a steely gaze.

"Matthews?" Laura asked with a confused look.

"It's complicated but I need him to help me catch someone," Ken told her trying to reveal as little as possible but at least that much was true.

"I was going to be looking for him today, so you're in luck," Laura replied as she handed him the coffee he'd asked for.

"Thank heaven," Ken declared right before taking a sip of the coffee he needed so desperately. "Luca's got this contraption he makes coffee in… I can't figure it out, so this… this is great."

The car glided through the city streets, the morning sun casting long shadows across the pavement. The world outside was waking up—children playing in parks, joggers making their morning rounds, and the hum of daily life resuming its rhythm. But inside the car, an anxiousness simmered just below the surface.

Ken rubbed his temples, trying to push away the lingering fatigue, and as if another piece of the puzzle struck him like a lightbulb going off in his head, he pulled out his phone. Laura watched curiously, wondering what was going on in his head. Ken scrolled through some numbers and picked one. He waited anxiously for someone on the other end to pick up.

"It's Walsh, pass me through to homicide," he said to the voice on the other end of the line.

After a few seconds more, another voice answered, "Homicide."

"It's Walsh," he said sternly, "I want everyone out of the East End crime scene, clear the area. I want it to look like no one was ever there," he instructed, scanning the busy park as Laura drove past.

As he hung up the phone, Laura turned to him, her brow furrowing slightly. "What are you planning?" she asked, her voice calm but laced with concern.

Ken looked at her and shook his head. "I want you to have plausible deniability," he said, his tone leaving no room for argument.

She nodded, understanding the unspoken weight of his words. This was more than just another case, more than a routine investigation. Whatever Ken was dealing with, it was something she'd rather not question.

They pulled up in front of a series of garden apartments, once a charming retreat, they now stood as a decaying relic. The stucco facade was cracked and faded, revealing patches of exposed brick and weathered wood. Overgrown vines strangled the neglected flower beds, while the courtyard's dry, brittle grass and debris-filled fountain spoke of years of neglect. Almost every window was clouded with grime, some had cracked panes and rust stains streaked the walls beneath groaning air conditioning units.

"Give me a minute, I'll check if he's in. Lay low, if he sees you, I'd imagine we'd have to chase him down," Laura insisted as she got out of the car and shut the door behind her.

Ken observed as she climbed the stairs to the second level, stopping at an apartment door that appeared as worn and neglected as the rest of the complex. She knocked lightly and waited for a response, but ultimately peered through the window to no avail. Undeterred, she jiggled the doorknob with no luck and then searched for a key in all the usual hiding spots - under the mat, above the door frame - before finally finding one tucked away under a small flower pot on the windowsill. Turning back to Ken, she silently mouthed "Bingo" with a satisfied grin before slipping inside. After only a minute, she emerged from the apartment with a somber expression, shaking her head to indicate that Vito Matthews was not home.

Ken watched Laura descend the stairs and head back. She entered the car and slammed the door behind her. "Fuck," Ken said. "Obviously my paying him a visit didn't help."

She shook her head as she started the car. "If that didn't stop him, nothing will. I'm going to head over to Clover Park," she said, her tone matter-of-fact as she pulled away from the curb, her focus shifting to the next potential lead.

The car glided through the streets, the city blurring past them as they moved with purpose. "Any word on the civil commitment for him?" Ken asked, trying to gauge the situation, while his mind was off in a different direction trying to piece together the fragments of the night.

Laura shook her head again, her lips pressing into a thin line. "I'm anxious to get him off the streets" she said, her voice taking on a slightly harder edge, the urgency of their mission clear.

Ken nodded, his mind already working through the next steps, the pieces of the puzzle slowly coming together in his mind. "Look, I won't ask what you're doing but you're not going at this alone, are you? Where's your partner?" Laura asked, glancing at him out of the corner of her eye, her curiosity piqued by the unspoken trust between them.

Ken hesitated, unsure of how to answer, the weight of Luca's absence hanging over him. "He's… working on it from another angle," he replied, his voice trailing off as he considered Luca's situation, the uncertainty gnawing at him.

Laura's gaze remained on the road, but there was a curious note in her voice as she asked, "You mind if I ask you an unrelated question? Laura said with some hesitation in her voice.

"Of course," Ken answered, now curious at this new line of questioning.

"Does he ask about me?" She finally spit out.

Ken gave her a double take. That question was probably as far out in left field as possible, catching him off guard. "Marchetti?" he echoed, a slight questioning crease spread across his brow as he tried to process the shift into the conversation.

"Yeah, has he ever, you know, mentioned me?" Laura asked, her tone casual, but there was a hint of something more hiding under the surface, something that hadn't been there before.

Ken glanced at her, his mind finally catching up. "You and Marchetti?" he asked, his voice tinged with disbelief, the idea seeming almost absurd in the midst of everything else.

Laura shrugged, a small smile playing on her lips as she kept her focus on the road. "I kinda got a thing for that priest vibe and all," she admitted, her tone light but sincere, the moment a brief reprieve from the tense car ride.

Ken gave her a look of utter bewilderment, his mind still not grasping the absurdity of it all, the juxtaposition of normalcy and the madness they were dealing with. "I… I'll have to get back to you on that," he said, his tone bemused, unsure of how to respond.

But then, as they approached Clover Park, Laura's focus sharpened as she surveyed the area. "Bingo," she said softly, her voice filled with quiet triumph.

Ken followed her gaze and spotted the man they had been searching for—Vito Matthews. He was lurking in the shadows on the sidewalk at the edge of the park, a sinister grin plastered across his face, his unkempt appearance giving him a predatory aura. His eyes were locked on the children playing at the edge of their parent's watchful gazes, a disturbing glimmer of twisted delight shining in their depths. The way he moved, with calculated steps and a slyness to his stance, made Ken's skin crawl. It was clear that Vito was up to no good, and Ken knew they needed to act fast before anyone got hurt.

"He's got a goddamn death wish," Laura muttered, her voice filled with disdain as she pulled the car to a stop, as she locked in on Vito.

Ken nodded as he watched Vito's every move. "You know what they say, 'be careful what you wish for,'" he replied, his tone unsettling, the implications clear.

A sense of danger pulsed through Vito as he glimpsed the car approaching. With a surge of adrenaline, he took off running, his movements frantic and uncoordinated. Laura wasted no time in pursuing him, pressing her foot down on the gas pedal and causing the car to lurch forward. The sound of the engine roared in Vito's ears as he sprinted ahead, his mind racing with thoughts of escape.

As he looked over his shoulder back at Laura's car, his shoulder clipped a light post sending him reeling in pain. He snapped to and crashed into a pedestrian that had his head buried in his cell phone. "Watch it man!" The pedestrian yelled in frustration." Vito didn't give the pedestrian a second look, his sole objective was to get away as he could sense Laura's car gaining on him.

He pressed on, dodging trash cans and the occasional bench and empty shopping cart. But as hard as he tried, he was no match for his own exhaustion; within the first hundred yards, his lungs were burning, and his legs felt like lead weights, thwarting his attempt to outrun his pursuer.

Laura slammed on the brakes, causing the car's tires to screech and smoke as she skidded to a stop next to Vito. She leapt out of the vehicle, her movements quick and purposeful. Vito became even more frantic as he watched Laura approach with single-mindedness etched across her face. His mind turned, trying desperately to come up with an excuse before she reached him.

"I wasn't doing anything, I swear!" Vito pleaded, his voice high-pitched and desperate as he tried to back away, his hands raised in a futile gesture of surrender. "I was just getting some air, I can get air can't I?" He continued in protest.

Ken strode around the car with calculated movements, his stare icy and unblinking as he locked onto Vito. Vito felt a shiver run down his spine as he recognized the intimidating presence of his antagonist. In a desperate attempt to escape, he tried to run again, but before he could take a step, Laura was upon him. With swift precision, she grabbed hold of his shirt collar and brought him crashing to the ground in one fluid motion. She stood over Matthews, as Ken moved in closer with an air of danger surrounding him. Fear pulsed through Vito's veins as he realized there was no escaping this confrontation.

"It looks like you won a ride downtown, Matthews," Ken said, his voice calm but laced with menace, the words stabbing into Matthews like a blade.

Vito's panicked voice rose above the chaos, a mix of terror and defiance as he struggled. He looked around frantically, searching for any means of escape from the looming threat that stood before him. "No, fuck man, come on! Get him away from me, that's police brutality! I want my attorney!" He cried out to Laura, desperation evident in every trembling word. Vito could feel Ken closing in on him like a noose.

Ken crouched down next to him, his voice dropping to a deadly whisper. "If you don't get your ass into that car, you will become the definition of police brutality when they look it up on Wikipedia," he said, his tone icy and unwavering, the threat palpable.

Vito's bravado crumbled instantly, his defiance giving way to pure terror. "Alright! Alright!" he stammered, scrambling to his feet. Laura handcuffed him and shoved him into the back seat of her car.

Ken slammed the rear door shut, narrowly missing Vito Matthew's head, startling him. He looked up through the passenger window up at Ken, and for the first time, he regretted the choice he made to leave his house that morning.

Without a word, Laura started up the vehicle and took off.

"Keep driving straight, I'll tell you where to turn," He told Laura in a soft but stern tone.

She looked at him inquisitively and just nodded back in agreement.

The car cruised through the city streets, the feeling inside tense and silent. Vito shifted nervously in the back seat, his focus darting around as he tried to figure out where they were taking him. The city passed by in a blur, but nothing looked familiar. His panic began to build as he realized they weren't heading toward the precinct.

"Where are you taking me?" Vito asked, his voice quivering with insecurity, his fright palpable in every word.

Both Laura and Ken ignored him, their focus locked on the road ahead. Vito's anxiety spiked, his voice rising in desperation. "Hey! This ain't the way to the precinct, where the hell are we going?"

Ken's brow furrowed with irritation as he turned slightly in his seat. "Another word, Vito. Just say one more word, and Weston here is gonna pull the car over, and you and I are going to continue our little chat from the other day," he warned, his tone deadly serious, leaving no doubt about what would happen next.

Vito's voice faded away as his anxiety took over, the car continued on its journey with an unknown destination and unbearable suspense. The cityscape turned more ominous as they drew near the east side of town, where Ken was leading Laura to the Hag's hideout.

Laura glanced in the rearview mirror and looked at Vito. "You're in for a rough ride, Matthews," she thought as she imagined the justice he would bring to this predator.

Laura's car rolled to a stop at the curb, the tires crunching over the gravel with a sound that seemed to shatter the heavy stillness clinging to the neighborhood. It was the kind of silence that felt unnatural, like the whole world stopped, waiting for something to happen.

The midday sun hung high in the sky, a merciless eye that cast stark unforgiving shadows across the cracked pavement. Everything seemed too bright, almost painfully so, as if the sun was trying to bleach away the memories of what had happened here, to scrub clean the stains that ran far deeper than blood.

The Hag's row-house stood in front of them looking less chilling in the daylight, it stood amongst others that had succumbed to a similar fate. Its once vibrant red brick façade had crumbled into shades of rust and ash, overtaken by the relentless growth of creeping ivy and the heavy soot from long-dead factories. The windows, now shattered and boarded up, gaped like hollow eyes, their frames warped and twisted with age. A rusted fire escape clung to the side of the building like a remnant of a bygone era when life pulsed through the narrow streets.

This was a place forgotten by time, a mere ghost of the city's former self. It held nothing but faded memories of what once was, slowly sinking deeper into oblivion.

The yellow police tape that had once served as a flimsy barrier against the horrors inside was now gone, leaving behind only the hollow shell of a place that had seen too much. There were no signs left of the police ever being there as if the world wanted to deny it happened, to forget that a house could hold such secrets within its decaying walls.

Laura stepped out of the car, her face a carefully controlled mask, but it betrayed a trace of concern. She turned her gaze to Ken.

"I have to be honest, Ken. I'm not comfortable leaving you here without backup," she said firmly. "I'll get a patrol assigned and make sure they stay out of your way."

Ken hesitated, knowing his plan could go awry if others got involved. He also knew that explaining it to Laura would be futile - either she wouldn't understand or she wouldn't allow it. "Luca is meeting me," he blurted out, staring straight at her. He was shocked that the response came so quick to his lips.

"You promise?" She demanded, not taking her eyes of his.

"I promise, he'll be here," Ken reassured her. And once again, he was being honest, although it was a convoluted truth that he could never fully explain.

She nodded, wanting to believe him. And with that she flung open the trunk. The loud metallic clang echoed through the eerie stillness, each noise magnified to an almost unbearable level. She grabbed the defibrillator case, flashlight, and police-grade zip ties, while Ken swiftly released Matthews from his handcuffs. They seamlessly traded items, with Laura taking the handcuffs and securing them onto her belt, and Ken taking the case

"You will call if you need me," she said, more an order than a question, her voice softening just a fraction.

Ken nodded a brief expression of gratitude before he refocused on the task at hand. Laura walked away, climbing back into her car. She paused for a moment, gripping the steering wheel tightly as she started the engine. Her gaze lingered on Ken, silently acknowledging their shared secret before she drove off into the sweltering heat, disappearing down the desolate road leaving Ken and Vito alone in the forgotten part of town.

Vito watched the car disappear, his nerves unraveling with each second. "Why is she leaving?" he asked, his voice trembling, desperation creeping in.

Ken remained silent, his jaw clenching tightly as he grabbed Vito by the back of the neck with a grip that could have crushed steel. With a rough shove, he propelled Vito forward, causing him to stumble. A sinking feeling settled in Vito's stomach as he realized he was completely at Ken's mercy. Panic set in as his mind raced with thoughts of what torment lay ahead for him, his dismay tangible. Vito braced himself for whatever was to come.

"Where's she going?" He repeated, his voice pitched higher, panic lacing every word. The neighborhood seemed to close in on them, growing more foreboding, more sinister.

Ken remained silent, his grip becoming tighter as he dragged Vito toward the Hag's row house. There was no room for hesitation, no room for mercy.

"Wha the hell is this place?" Vito complained as he took in the rundown building in front of him.

Without a word, Ken shoved Vito through the front door, the man's body crashing to the floor with a flat unsettling thump.

The musty smell of death filled their nostrils as they made their way deeper inside. Sunlight barely trickled in through the broken windows, painting a sickly glow on the decaying furniture and moldy carpet. Vito couldn't shake off the feeling that something sinister was hidden in there, waiting to pounce.

The great room of the row house had transformed from mere neglect to something far more sinister. In one corner, a rough-hewn wooden table with a myriad of rusted tools that looked like they were straight out of medieval torture chamber. Above the table, scrawled crudely onto the cracked plaster wall, was the large pentagram, the lines uneven but unmistakable. Dark, oily smears of what could only be blood traced the symbol, the blackened residue suggesting ritual use over countless nights. The sight of it seemed to hum with a dark energy, a silent scream vibrating through the walls.

Cobwebs hung thick in every corner, their delicate strands swaying as though disturbed by an unseen presence. The floorboards creaked beneath the weight of the two men as cockroaches skittered on the ground next to Vito's face. The air was thick with a suffocating dread, as if the very house had become a living thing, feeding off the dark energy that had taken residence within its crumbling walls.

On a nearby shelf, strange totems and objects—animal bones, feathers, and jars filled with strange, unidentifiable substances—lay scattered. Each piece looked as though it had been used in rituals long forgotten by the world outside. The room had become a temple to darkness, a place where the boundaries between the living and the dead had long since blurred.

Vito scrambled to his feet, a whimper escaping his throat as his gaze landed on a nearby shelf. Six heads stared back at him, their sockets vacant, flesh torn and mutilated. The tableau of death froze him in place, a high-pitched squeal escaping his lips.

"Oh God, no, what is this!? What the hell is this!?" Vito cried, his voice cracking under the strain of sheer terror.

In a split second, before Vito could even form another word, Ken's fist swung violently towards him. The impact was merciless and unrelenting, sending Vito crashing to the floor once again, the sound of his body hitting the ground echoing through the room. His vision was engulfed in a dazzling burst of stars until finally everything went black.

CHAPTER 16

VENGEANCE UNLEASHED

As Vito stirred, a fierce pain throbbed through his head, spreading like wildfire. The emptiness surrounding him was suffocating, a black veil that seemed to smother every sound and movement. He blinked, struggling to adjust to the emptiness, but it was futile—the room remained an abyss of nothingness. Whatever little light that had been there earlier was now gone. His thoughts were muddled and disoriented, trying to piece together where he was and how he had ended up here.

He attempted to move, but his body was bound tightly with unforgiving zip ties that dug into his skin like fangs. Panic edged its way through his chest, his thoughts racing wildly as he fought against the restraints. The plastic dug deeper into his flesh, drawing droplets of crimson blood. And in one sudden realization, all the memories came rushing back to him in a torrential flood.

"Detective?" Vito's voice trembled. The name was a desperate plea for help that wouldn't come. The stench hit him full force—decay, sweat, something worse. It turned his stomach, bile rising in his throat. "Oh, God," he muttered, gagging, his body convulsing with the effort to keep the contents of his stomach down.

He struggled harder, frantic, but the ties held firm. Panic blooming into full-blown terror. "Detective!" Vito screamed, his voice echoing off the grimy walls. "Someone help me!" he cried, his voice breaking, raw with desperation.

A voice cut through the nothingness—cold, detached. "Nobody for miles, Vito. You're alone. Just you and me... for now."

Vito's entire body froze, every muscle stiffening in shock. The blood drained from his face, leaving it pale. He strained to see through the darkness, searching desperately for any sign of Ken's presence, but it was no use. It was as if he had disappeared into the shadows. "I-I never laid a hand on any kid!" Vito blurted out, his voice trembling with angst and confusion. But his protest sounded weak and insincere, lacking conviction even to himself. They were just words, hollow and empty, unable to erase the guilt and shame that consumed him.

Ken stepped forward, and even though Vito couldn't see him, his presence loomed like a specter of judgment. "I've seen the surveillance tapes," he said, his voice low, dangerous. "Lie to me again, and I'll enjoy ripping your tongue out."

"You can't do this! You're a cop!" Vito's voice cracked, desperation seeping into every syllable.

Ken's calm demeanor was unnerving, his detachment sending shivers down Vito's spine. "Good cops play by the rules, that's for sure," he began, his voice low and controlled. "But a father...a father plays by different rules." He paused, his stare boring into Vito's with intense fury. "Rules that you wouldn't understand." His words were like daggers, each one punctuated by his unwavering gaze. "I have a little girl," he continued, his voice dropping to a whisper laced with emotion. "She once met a man like you. The intensity in Ken's voice grew sharper as he spoke. "The confusion of what happened gives her nightmares to this day." He paused, his jaw clenching as he relived painful memories. "Unfortunately, that man took the easy way out - pills, quietly fading away without letting justice take its course." A violent edge crept into Ken's tone. "He didn't deserve peace. None of you deserve peace."

"Please…" Vito's voice broke, a pitiful whimper as he struggled against the zip ties, the plastic digging deeper, blood pooling at his wrists.

Ken's steps resonated through the silence, each creaking floorboard adding to the tension in the air. "I won't lay a another finger on you, Vito," his voice was barely audible, but it held a sense of danger and boldness. Ken flicked on his flashlight, the beam harsh, spotlighting Vito, who flinched, squinting against the brightness. Ken's face was hard, devoid of mercy, staring at Vito with an intensity that made the man's blood run cold.

"What is coming, is worse than you can ever imagine," Ken warned, his tone reflected a hint of horror and foreboding, a glimpse into the terror he had witnessed. "An evil you've never dreamed of." The weight of those words hung heavy in the night air, filling Vito with a sense of alarm.

Vito's sobs intensified, his body convulsing as he fought the restraints, pain mingling with terror. "I'll go to treatment! I'll confess! Please, I swear! I got money, you want money? I'll do anything!" His voice was a desperate plea, but Ken remained unmoved, the cold detachment reflecting the depth of his resolve.

"You're doing exactly what I need you to do," Ken murmured, his voice frigid, disconnected, as he patted Vito's cheek with calculated indifference. Then he stepped back, switching off the flashlight, plunging the room into a blackness neither one of them had ever experienced.

Vito's muffled sobs filled the room, raw, desperate, echoing off the walls. "Please, why, why are you doing this?" Vito begged as Ken faded into the shadows, his presence barely perceptible, a ghost in the night, watching, waiting.

"I needed a pig," Ken's voice emerged from the black, cold and distant, like a judgment passed down from the ether.

Vito thrashed in the chair, the restraints now deeper, his skin rubbed raw, bleeding. He was trapped, helpless, a cornered animal, every instinct screaming at him to flee, to fight, but there was no escape.

A loud THUMP reverberated through the room, freezing Vito in place. The noise came from the rickety roof above their heads. The rush of blood in his ears drowned out all rational thought, leaving him with nothing but the primal instinct to survive. Heavy footsteps echoed from above, slow, deliberate, like the approach of death itself. Someone—or something—was coming. Vito looked around frantically, trying to see what was coming for him.

THUD! The noise moved just outside the door, it was heavy, making the rickety door rattle from the impact. Vito's mind reeled with terror, his throat constricted, squeezing out the oxygen.

Ken watched anxiously, moving his hand swiftly to the defibrillator. He found the switch, and flipped it on. The machine hummed to life, the high-pitched whine breaking through the silence, a sharp contrast to the restrictive stillness that filled the room.

The footsteps drew nearer, each one measured, purposeful, echoing from the outside with a cadence that made Vito's body tremble. He pulled against the restraints, the pain now secondary to the overwhelming terror flooding his senses. The footsteps stopped just outside the door, the air crackled with anticipation, every muscle in Vito's body tense, waiting for the inevitable.

The door groaned open, its slow movements breaking the silence with a jarring finality. A figure emerged, towering over the crumbling surroundings. The Hag loomed in the moonlight, her silhouette barely visible but her gaze piercing through the darkness. Vito could feel her eyes fixed on him, their intensity sending chills down his spine. As she moved closer, her actions calculated and precise, Vito's fear only grew.

Ken's grip tightened around the defibrillator paddles, his knuckles turning white from the pressure. He was nervous, but determined to stay alert. This was his chance to end this nightmare once and for all.

The Hag tilted her head as she surveyed the scene in front of her. She sensed an ambush, but it only excited her further, drawing her deeper into her lair. Her confidence in her own viciousness never wavered; she had faced centuries of conflict and always emerged victorious. Each step she took landed with a quiet grace, yet it carried a weight that rippled through the room, undeniable, like a storm gathering on the horizon. It wasn't just the way she moved—fluid and sure—it was something deeper, something primal. An aura of certainty surrounded her, as if she knew things others couldn't even guess at. She didn't demand attention; she simply drew it, like gravity pulling everything into her orbit. You couldn't help but watch, mesmerized, by both fear, and the strange sense that in her presence, the world itself might shift.

With the strike of a match, she lit a hurricane lamp on a nearby table, casting a flickering light through a small section of the room. The flame revealed her terrifying appearance - tattered clothes, sunken cheeks, jagged teeth glinting in the dim light. The space was bathed in an eerie glow, exposing the decay and grime that covered every surface. And there sat Vito, tied to a chair like a helpless rat caught in a trap. His eyes widened with shock and horror

And out of the darkness Ken stepped in to the light, defibrillator paddles in hand.

"Your Royal Highness," He said with grim sarcasm, his voice steady as he jammed the paddles into her bony chest and pressed the trigger button.

With a sudden jolt, the defibrillator discharged, sending a powerful surge of electricity into the Hag's body. Her limbs thrashed and contorted in agony, her twisted features distorting even further as the voltage coursed through her. The air pulsed with an electric charge, causing the hair on the back of Ken's neck to stand on end and his skin to tingle with energy. But just as quickly as it came, the thrashing stopped and she stood upright in a strange unnatural manner, her eyes blazing with hatred as she fixed her gaze on Ken.

Ken's heart sank as the Hag stared at him, baring her teeth like a rabid wolf. He had been sure that a jolt of a thousand volts would stop her rancid heart from beating. But looking at the display on the machine, he felt a heavy sense of dread wash over him. The word "CHARGING" mocked his haste and lack of preparation in bold letters. Panic surged through him as he realized the paddles had not been fully charged and time was running out. Sweat dripped down his temples as the Hag moved with surprising agility despite her twisted figure. She snarled fiercely and struck Ken with a backhand, sending him crashing into the solid brick wall behind him. Pain shot through his body as he hit the unyielding surface, knocking the wind out of him and leaving him vulnerable and disoriented. As he struggled to regain his senses, he realized the defibrillator paddles had slipped just out of reach.

The Hag's attention shifted to Vito, who was trembling uncontrollably in the chair with unbridled terror. She stepped towards him with slow, deliberate movements, relishing the fear that radiated off of him like an intoxicating scent. Her long, bony fingers reached out and grabbed his cheek, digging into his flesh with sharp claws. She leaned in closer, her nose twitching as she greedily inhaled the pungent smell of his terror. "Mmmm," she hummed with satisfaction, pleased with her find - a pedophile's meat ripe for the taking. The distress emanating from Vito only made her more powerful and she reveled in it, knowing she would consume him at any moment.

The compilation of foul scents now included the stench of urine as Vito lost control, a pool of liquid forming beneath the rickety chair, his body betraying him. The Hag, her wrinkled skin glistening with sweat and grime, stuck her long bony finger into his mouth grabbing at his tongue with a sudden jerk, causing Vito's already swollen and bruised lips to split open and bleed profusely. Then she leaned in close enough for Vito to feel her hot, rancid breath on his face as she cackled maniacally and flicked her tongue onto his as if she was tasting him.

Without warning, she bared her yellowed teeth and sunk them into Vito's cheek with a sickening crunch. He screamed a high-pitched, agonizing wail that filled the room with the sound of his suffering. His blood mixed with his tears as it poured from the gaping wound, staining his face and clothes.

The Hag chewed the chunk of flesh with fervor, her lips smacking as blood poured out of Vito's face while she savored her meal. She had an undeniable expression of sadistic pleasure reveling in his pain and terror. To her, this was just another day at work - an offering to the demons that kept her alive. And poor Vito was just another helpless victim in her clutches.

Vito's screams were primal and jarring, his voice raw with terror as he desperately tried to break free from her grasp. His mind was fractured, shattered by the sheer horror of his situation. In one final, desperate attempt, he flung himself at the Hag, head-butting her with all his remaining strength. For a brief moment, she was taken aback, shocked by his sudden burst of opposition.

The Hag recoiled slightly, her head tilting as if considering this unexpected resistance, a twisted smile creeping across her face. Then, she spoke in that chilling, sing-song voice, "Mary, Mary, quite contrary…"

In one swift, savage movement, she struck Vito hard across the face, sending him and the chair tumbling to the ground in a cacophony of crashing wood. As he hit the floor with a bone-jarring thud, he could feel the searing pain radiating through his body from the shattered chair beneath him. A shrill, deafening noise pierced his ears, amplifying the agonizing sensation as he struggled to even lift a hand in defense.

The Hag's voice erupted from deep within her, a violent scream that shook the very foundations of the house. The walls trembled with its intensity. Vito, now on the ground amidst the squalor that lay on the floor, was reduced to incoherent blubbering, his mind teetering on the edge of madness, consumed by the terror that pulsed through his veins.

In a desperate plea for help, Vito managed to utter, "Somebody... please!"

But the Hag showed no mercy. She smiled as she lifted her machete high above her head, preparing to strike down upon him. With a twisted smile on her face, she taunted him with the eerie rhyme, "How does your garden grow..."

Vito's every sense was overwhelmed with the impending doom as the Hag's blade glinted in the dull light from the hurricane lamp. Panic and pain clouded Vito's mind as he braced himself for the strike that would end his life.

A loud sound echoed from behind her- it was Ken, groaning in pain as he struggled to stand. His vision blurred and his body ached, but his mind was solely focused on surviving the encounter. He saw the Hag's back turned towards him and knew this may be his only chance. As she turned to face him with her head cocked at an odd angle, Ken reached for his gun with trembling hands. But something made him hesitate. The high-pitched whine of the defibrillator filled the room once again, reminding him of his mission.

"Luca..." Ken whispered a plea to his fallen friend and a prayer to whatever higher power could assist him now.

Ken's trembling hands quickly holstered his gun and he turned to find the defibrillator. The machine hummed loudly, its digital levels glaring at him with a sense of urgency: "CHARGING."

He scrambled towards it and managed to grab the paddles while simultaneously knocking over everything in his path.

The Hag charged towards him. And at that moment, time seemed to slow down as Ken desperately tried to remember what to do next. Everything moved in slow motion, like a scene out of a movie. And in the last second, amidst the chaos and adrenaline, the machine's beeps switched from "Charging" to "Charged." A glimmer of hope sparked within Ken as he knew this could be their only chance to survive.

The deafening CRACK of 1,000 volts echoed through the room as it struck the Hag square in the chest. She was hurled backward, her body contorted and flailing as she crashed into the opposite wall before slumping to the ground in a twisted heap. But Ken knew this wasn't enough to defeat her - her evil was too deeply rooted, too powerful to be vanquished so easily.

Ken reached for the defibrillator once more. The chaos around him seemed to fade into the background as he focused on his task. He stepped over Vito, who was still writhing on the floor and positioned himself to deliver another jolt to the Hag. His hands were steady despite the adrenaline coursing through his veins and he was ready to do whatever it took to rid the world of her wickedness.

"Just shoot her!!" Vito screamed hysterically, his voice laced with terror. His bloody and torn hands finally managing to slip through the zip ties, leaving his skin raw and ragged. His ankles broke free from under the chair legs and he scrambled to his feet. The screeching sound of the defibrillator grew louder once again. Ken stared intently at the machine, holding his breath in anticipation for it to charge. "Hurry up, hurry up, hurry up!" he mumbled urgently, the tension evident in his voice.

Beep!

Ken looked down at the Hag, his voice flat and resolute. "Sorry, Luca."

As another 1,000 volts of electricity surged into the demonic being, a deafening CRACK echoed through the room. Her contorted body writhed on the ground before finally falling still and lifeless. The air was thick with the acrid smell of burnt flesh.

For a brief moment, a heavy silence settled over the room. But it was short-lived as Vito, consumed by a potent mix of fear and rage, let out a primal scream and swung what was left of the chair with all his might onto Ken's back. The sound of splintering wood filled the room as the chair connected with a stomach turning thud. With a pained groan, Ken crumpled to the ground, his body unable to withstand the force of the blow. In that split second, any sense of control and composure that Vito might have had shattered in a burst of violence and chaos.

"You psychotic bastard!" He shouted, his voice laced with hysteria. He raised the broken chair above his head and brought it crashing down again and again, each strike fueled by a dangerous mix of terror and madness.

"I'll kill you, you fucking animal!" Vito roared, his voice breaking as he continued to pummel Ken with the broken pieces of the chair. The room echoed with the sound of wood splintering and Vito's ragged breathing as he stood over Ken, gripping a jagged piece of chair leg in his hand. His eyes were wild, his face twisted with unbridled fury.

"Scum!" Vito screamed, thrusting the makeshift stake into Ken's shoulder. Blood gushed from the wound, crimson and thick, staining Ken's shirt."Fuck you!" Vito snarled, raising the stake for another strike. As he brought it down, a hand reached up and grabbed him by the groin.

The Hag's hand, gnarled and icy, hooked into Vito's crotch with an iron grip. He let out another piercing scream that was so loud the sound might have been heard blocks away. The pain shot through him like a wave of fire, igniting every nerve in his body and leaving him writhing in agony. The Hag's nails dug deeper, drawing blood and leaving behind deep gashes in his flesh. Every ounce of strength seemed to drain from his body as he struggled to break free from her grasp. But the Hag held on, relentless in her torment. Vito could feel his body going numb, the pain almost too much to bear. Blood seeped through his pants, staining the fabric crimson as she continued to squeeze.

Vito's grip weakened, the stake slipped from his bloodied fingers as his body convulsed in agony. He fell to his knees, his face twisted in a grimace of pain and terror. His muscles twitched and spasmed uncontrollably, sweat beading on his forehead as he stared into nothingness his mind shattering under the intense pressure of the Hag's hold. Drool dripped from his parted lips, a sign of his complete and utter defeat at the hands of the powerful witch.

The high-pitched whine of the defibrillator machine filled the room again, severing the muddy atmosphere like a blade.

Beep!

The Hag's body slackened, her grotesque features softening as the last of her depraved life force drained away. Her hand fell limp from Vito's crotch, releasing him from her vice-like grasp.

Ken came to, his vision clouded by a haze of pain. His head throbbed mercilessly from the brutal attack. With a groan, he attempted to push himself up, but every movement sent a jolt of agony through his body. His shoulder cried in objection where the sharp stake had pierced his flesh. Every inch of him was battered and bruised, the result of the vicious beating he had endured. As he struggled to stand, he felt muscles he never knew existed screaming in protest. He glanced at Vito, who lay convulsing on the ground, blood pooling beneath him. Nearby, Luca lay motionless and eerily quiet, his friend's body now limp and broken.

With his body aching and battered, Ken mustered all of his remaining strength to pull himself upright. Every step towards Luca was an agonizing struggle, but he knew he had to keep going.

His fingers trembling from exhaustion and adrenaline, sweat poured down his forehead and stung as it went into the lacerations on it. He hastily unbuttoned Luca's shirt, revealing the bruised and bloodied skin beneath. His body was pale and motionless, and Luca looked like a fragile porcelain doll in Ken's hands.

With determination carved onto his face, he placed the defibrillator paddles on Luca's bare chest, praying for a miracle.

"Come on, Luca," he muttered through gritted teeth, flicking on the switch. "You're not going out like this!"

ZAP!

He zapped his friend and watched the electricity surge through Luca's body forcing it to buckle upwards in an abnormally high arch. As his body settled back down, Ken checked for a pulse, but there was nothing. Panic rose in his throat as he frantically searched for any sign of life.

But then it hit him—the defibrillator hadn't worked. He had killed Luca.

Tears welled up as he fell to his knees beside the lifeless body before him. "I killed a fucking priest," he uttered in disbelief, the weight of his actions crashing down on him.

BEEP. The single beep cut through the silence. And with renewed determination, Ken steadied himself, his hands trembling as he prepared to zap Luca once more. The metallic paddles felt cold and foreign in his grasp, a stark contrast to the warm blood coating his fingers. "Come on, come on, come on!" he urged with desperation lacing his voice as he slammed the paddles down on Luca's chest.

There was a loud zap followed by a familiar thudding noise.

The sound echoed through the room, bouncing off the walls and filling the air with an eerie stillness. Ken's head snapped up at the sudden noise. Vito was somehow back on his feet, and was repeatedly smashing his head against the wall with unnatural force. Each impact sent shivers down Ken's spine, and he couldn't help but feel a sinking sense of impending doom.

THUMP!

Vito rotated slowly, his movements stiff and robotic, as if something evil was pulling the strings. His face was a gruesome sight, with chunks of flesh ripped away to reveal a distorted grin that sent shivers down Ken's spine. His gaze was hollow and expressionless, devoid of all humanity.

Ken felt the rush of anxiety creep up his spine as he realized what had happened. He watched in terror as Vito scanned the room like he was a computer rebooting and slowly coming back online. Vito's lips curled back, revealing jagged teeth stained with blood as he opened his mouth wide and unleashed that primal scream that pulsated through his bones. It was a sound of pure torment and malice, striking terror into Ken's very soul.

Vito turned fully toward Ken, his posture stiff and unnatural as if he were being controlled by some unseen force. Then, from the far end of the room, the machete flew into Vito's hand like Thor's hammer returning to its owner. Vito raised the blade high above his head, morphing completely into the Hag as his scream echoed in Ken's ears.

Ken fumbled for his gun, but his holster was empty. It had fallen during the scuffle, but where? Instinctively, Ken raised his good arm to shield himself from the incoming blow but he knew it was futile. He had lost everything, his family, his friend, and the battle to rid the world of the evil that stood before him. As the machete came down, a series of deafening gunshots rang out.

BAM! BAM! BAM!

The bullets hit Vito the Hag, square in the forehead, the force of the impact sending him sprawling backward and forcing the blade to just miss Ken's arm by a fraction of an inch. Vito dropped like a sack of potatoes, the machete clattering to the floor beside him. Blood pooled beneath his motionless body, spreading across the filthy floorboards.

Ken was shocked as he turned to see Luca crouched and holding his gun, the barrel still smoking from the shots. Luca's face was pale, his expression one of grim determination. He stepped forward his movements deliberate as he unloaded the remaining rounds into the Hag's lifeless body.

BAM! BAM! BAM!

Luca's hand shook as he lowered the gun. He stared at the Hag's body lying there, his mind reeling, not knowing how he had gotten there and why. "What the hell happened?" Luca asked, his voice shaky, as he glanced at Ken with a look of confusion.

Ken, still dazed from the shock of the events, managed a grim smile. "I think I found Jesus," he said, his voice heavy with irony, "and you finally used a service weapon."

Luca's gaze fixed on the gun in his palm; he couldn't believe it was there. He had no recollection of grabbing it. It was as if he had been absent from his body and suddenly regained consciousness to find himself holding the weapon. He shook his head, trying to make sense of the missing moments. All he could recall was the altercation in the alleyway before everything went blank.

Luca handed the gun back to Ken and walked over to the Hag's body. His expression hardened as he grabbed the machete from the floor.

"What are you doing?!" Ken exclaimed, alarmed as he watched Luca. "Stay away from her!"

Luca ignored his friend and began hacking away at the Hag's hands, the blade slicing through flesh and bone with disturbing accuracy.

"I'm making sure this ends here," Luca said, gritting his teeth, his voice cold and emotionless.

Ken watched, his own expression blank, absent of any remorse or horror. They had crossed a line tonight, and there was no going back.

For a long moment, Ken and Luca stood in the dimly lit room, surrounded by the remnants of the horror they had just survived. Blood stained the floor, the walls, and their clothes. But they were alive. The two men exchanged a glance, a silent understanding passing between them. They had fought the devil and survived—barely.

Ken holstered his gun and nodded to Luca, his expression weary but resolute. "Let's get the hell out of here," he said, his voice hoarse.

Luca didn't respond, but he didn't need to. Together, they turned their backs on the hovel, stepping out into the night, and for the first time in what felt like an eternity, life seemed less unbearable.

But as they walked away, the dilapidated row house loomed behind them, its windows watching them like a silent reminder of the evil they had faced. The danger may have retreated for now, but it would never truly be gone. It lingered in the corners of the city, waiting for the next chance to strike.

CHAPTER 17

JUST OKAY

Three days had passed since the Hag had been shoved into a morgue freezer although it felt like years since both Luca and Ken had this kind of uninterrupted sleep. The clean, soothing coolness of Luca's apartment was broken up only by the soft, warm glow of a single lamp, illuminating a small corner of the room. The silence was peaceful, almost tangible, wrapping itself around him like a comforting blanket, offering a brief moment of solace.

After what seemed like an eternity, Ken's breathing finally calmed. His chest rose and fell in a steady pattern, and his injured face relaxed as sleep started to overtake him. As he drifted into slumber, the traumas of the night disappeared, replaced by a peaceful emptiness where nightmares were forbidden to enter.

But peace was a fleeting luxury for someone like Ken, and after a couple of hours of the best sleep he had ever experienced, his phone buzzed.

The sharp vibration of the phone severed the quiet, jarring him from the depths of sleep. The device rattled on the coffee table, its incessant hum filling the room. Ken stirred, a low groan escaping his lips as his body protested the rude awakening. The tranquility that had just begun to soothe his battered mind shattered like glass.

BUZZ.

His eyes fluttered open, the remnants of sleep clinging stubbornly to him. The world was a blur as he squinted at the source of the noise. He reached out with a heavy hand and grabbed the phone, its cold surface almost alien in his groggy state. Bringing it to his ear, he forced himself to focus, though his voice was still coarse with exhaustion.

"Walsh," he muttered, his tone laced with irritation. He listened as the voice on the other end delivered the latest in what felt like an endless string of bad news. "Seriously, can't I get more than two nights in a row to rest?" he grumbled, rubbing a hand over his face in a futile attempt to wipe away the fatigue. The voice on the other end continued, and Ken's frustration grew. "Yeah, yeah, I'll be there."

He ended the call with a resigned sigh, tossing the phone back onto the table with a dull thud. For a moment, he simply sat there, staring blankly at the ceiling as the weight of his life bore down on him.

"I need a new fucking job," he muttered to himself, the words tinged with bitter irony. But deep down, he knew there was no running from this life. It was in his blood, as much a part of him as the air in his lungs.

The hallway outside Luca's room was poorly lit, the fading lightbulb overhead casting an uneven glow on the hardwood floors. Ken stood before the half-open door, his knuckles rapping lightly against the wood. The sound was muted, almost swallowed by the silence that pervaded the apartment at this late hour.

He pushed the door open a little farther, his breath catching as he peered inside. The room was softly lit by a solitary bedside lamp, its amber light casting gentle shadows that danced across the walls. Luca lay on the bed, his back turned toward the door —a picture of tranquility amid the turbulence that so often defined their world. Beside him was a woman whose curly chestnut hair flowed down her bare back, the locks catching the warm glow and shimmering softly. Her clothes were scattered throughout the room, draped over chairs and tangled on the floor, as if a whirlwind had swept through and left fragments of the storm in its wake.

"Psst. Marchetti," Ken whispered, his voice barely more than a breath, as if even the darkness could be rattled by the sound. Luca stirred, a faint groan slipping from his lips—enough to show he was alive, but not nearly enough to signal interest. His body said it all: a heavy, deliberate stillness, a message as clear as if he'd spoken it out loud. He wasn't going to play along with whatever crisis Ken was dragging in from the night.

"Come on, man," Ken muttered, half pleading, half impatient. He waited, hoping for any sign that Luca would snap to, but instead, Luca shifted again, slower this time, pulling the pillow over his head with the lethargic defiance of someone who couldn't care less. One hand shot out from beneath the pillow, middle finger raised high, dismissing Ken and everything outside the door in a single gesture. The woman next to him stirred, murmuring something soft, and wrapped her arm lazily around his waist, anchoring him further in the cocoon of indifference.

Ken sighed, resigning himself to the fact that he wouldn't win this battle easily. He stepped back into the hallway, the door creaking slightly as he let it swing open just a bit more, allowing a sliver of light to spill into the room. He knew Luca would come around—he always did. But for now, there was nothing left to do but wait.

Ken wandered into Luca's small kitchen, a place that was both familiar and alien to him. The lure of coffee was the only thing that kept him focused. He fumbled with the mocha pot, trying to piece together the steps he'd seen Luca perform countless times. But fatigue dulled his mind, and his clumsy attempts only added to his frustration. This, too, felt like a battle he was destined to lose.

Luca shuffled into the kitchen, his hair a tousled mess, barely awake, yet somehow still managing to carry the same infuriating air of nonchalance. He paused in the doorway, leaning against the frame, watching Ken's struggles with a lazy smirk, his eyes half-lidded with sleep.

"Seriously?" Luca rasped, his voice rough from the night, yet edged with that familiar tone of teasing—equal parts amusement and gentle annoyance. It hit Ken like a low blow, irritating but strangely reassuring. Even in his groggy state, Luca had that way about him, making the smallest of moments feel like part of some ongoing joke only he was in on.

"There's a 1035 call," Ken explained, glancing up at Luca with a resigned look on his face. "Thought you might want to go for a ride."

Luca paused for a moment, tussled his hair, and then stared down his friend.

"Why the hell not?" Luca muttered, half to himself. "You woke me up, and I can't imagine getting back to sleep with you pouting like that."

He crossed the small kitchen in a few strides and snatched the coffee maker from Ken's hands. "I'll draw you a diagram for this thing so you can make coffee once in a while," he smirked.

"Uhhh..." Ken hesitated with the question that was on his lips.

"Yes?" Luca asked, eyebrows raised. "You're gonna ask at some point, so go ahead."

"How was it... when you changed?" Ken asked softly.

Luca stopped and thought for a second then he looked up at Ken.

"You don't have to tell me if you don't..." Ken offered as Luca cut him off.

"I've thought about it and it began as a whisper—so faint at first, I thought it was the wind, a rustle in the leaves. But no, it came from inside. Deep down, in the marrow of my bones. A voice, soft but persistent, threading its way through my thoughts like smoke. At first, I ignored it, told myself it was nothing. But it grew. It *grew*.

There was a moment, just before everything slipped away, when I still had control—when I could feel myself slipping but hadn't yet fallen. It was like standing at the edge of a cliff, the ground crumbling beneath my feet, the abyss yawning wide below. My heart raced, my skin crawled with a static electricity, and my hands—my own hands—felt foreign, as if they belonged to someone else.

Then it happened.

The voice wasn't a whisper anymore. It roared through me, drowning out everything else—my thoughts, my memories, the very essence of *me*. I tried to scream, but I imagine the sound never left my throat. I was still there, somewhere inside, I could see you there in the dark, but it was as if I were trapped behind glass, watching through my own eyes as something else —something *other*—took control. I could feel its hunger, its hatred, coursing through me like fire, filling my veins with a terrible, cold heat.

Every muscle twitched, every nerve sparked with a sick energy that wasn't mine. My body moved, but not at my command. My hands—the same hands that I was so used to—became unrecognizable claws, tearing at the world around me, at anyone foolish enough to come close. And the worst part? I didn't care. That small part of me, the one that still clung to the edges of who I used to be, was horrified, but I could feel the darkness inside me, a part of me relishing it.

I wasn't just a passenger in my own body anymore. I was *fading*. The line between me and it blurred until I wasn't sure where I ended and it began. All I knew was the hunger, the rage, the endless need to destroy, to consume. It was a dark, bottomless pit, and I was filled with the cold certainty that I would never be free again. Then you brought me back from eternal despair and I will never be able to thank you enough.

Ken nodded in understanding as Luca expression was of sheer gratitude.

"Coffee would help," Ken said with a genuine smile.

Luca smiled back, and with practiced ease, he unscrewed the top of the mocha coffee pot, his movements fluid and precise, honed by years of routine.

"By the way, is that Weston in there?" Ken asked with a knowing grin.

Luca smiled and shook his head. He wasn't going to answer that question but once again, all was right with the tumultuous world they lived in. With all its trials and tribulations, things were okay, and just "okay," was good enough for the two of them.

CHAPTER 18

ASHES AND ECHOES

The morgue was a place of sterile efficiency, the room cool and dry, laden with the scent of antiseptic and the faint, lingering odor of decay. The overhead fluorescent lights hummed softly, casting a harsh, clinical light over the room. Metal tables gleamed under the illumination, each one a cold, unforgiving slab that had borne witness to countless post-mortem examinations.

Mitch, was a man who had long since become desensitized to the grim tasks his job required. The cold metal handle felt unforgiving in his grip, almost like touching death itself. The morgue was quiet, save for the hum of the refrigeration units, a constant reminder of the temporary stillness death brings. With a practiced tug, the drawer slid out smoothly, a whisper of sound as the steel tracks groaned under the weight of the body.

There she was, wrapped in a pale sheet that seemed too thin to hold back the finality beneath it. The sterile chill from the cold chamber spilled out, mixing with the air in the room, a reminder that the body had been here longer than anyone cared to admit. Her tag dangled from her toe, swaying gently, like some kind of grim pendulum marking time's last breath.

He positioned the gurney beside the drawer, the click of its wheels the only sound breaking the silence. The body was heavy—not from weight, but from the sheer gravity of death itself. Lifting the sheet-wrapped figure took a steady hand and a strong back, but he moved with care, as if the still body could still feel the cold hands of the living. The muscles in his arms tightened as he guided the tray from the drawer onto the gurney, each movement precise and deliberate.

With a soft grunt, he secured the body in place, rolling it toward the examination table. There was always a strange tension in this part of the process, a brief moment when the body crossed from cold storage to the harsh light of examination. It was the transition from anonymity to revelation. What secrets had this body taken with it? What answers waited beneath the skin?

The gurney hit the examination table with a slight jolt, and he paused. Then, with the same deliberate motion, he shifted the body onto the table, the sheet crinkling softly as it settled. He pulled back the covering, revealing the face beneath. His breath halted at the sight. He had forgotten who this victim was and the pallor of death clung to her mangled skin, her grotesque face a waxen mask of what had once been life.

For a brief moment, he stood there, staring. It always struck him—this fragile line between the person they had been and the body they had become. Then, with a steadying breath, he reached for his tools, preparing to unlock the secrets hidden within that silent, still form.

With a scalpel in hand, Mitch scraped away at the remnants of brain matter clinging to the Hag's half-blasted forehead. The sharp blade sliced through the flesh with ease, separating the tissue from the bone in small, delicate strokes. The Hag's severed hands sat in a bowl nearby, and a toe tag dangled from her lifeless foot.

The room was eerily quiet, save for the faint rustle of Mitch's gloves and the occasional metallic clink of instruments against the metal tray beside him. He carefully placed the scrapings into a small, clear plastic cylinder, sealing it with a quick, efficient motion.

Mitch spoke into a recorder, his voice steady and detached, a professional tone honed over years of dispassionate observation.

"As I begin the external examination of the deceased, it's immediately apparent that there are three gunshot wounds located on the head. The entry wounds suggest the person was shot at close range, given the stippling present around the margins. All three of the bullets appear to have entered through the frontal region, indicating the same angle of fire."

He leaned closer to the corpse, his face inches from the grotesque injury where a large portion of the Hag's cheek had been torn away.

"Significant traumatic injury to the face is noted," Mitch continued, his voice calm, though his breath quivered with a hint of unease. "Specifically, a large portion of the left cheek is missing, consistent with being chewed off. The edges of the wound are jagged and uneven, suggesting a combination of tearing and biting force was applied."

As Mitch leaned in further, the stark reality of his words filled the air with a cold, clinical detachment. But then, something changed. The room seemed to grow colder, the lights dimming ever so slightly as if a grey swath of paint spread across the walls. The air felt electric, more alive, as if the very room was charged with an unseen energy.

The Hag's eyes snapped open, the lifelessness that once clouded them replaced by a cruel, fiendish gleam. Her neck lunged forward with a speed and ferocity that defied her previously lifeless state. Her rotted jaws snapped open, and before Mitch could react, the Hag sank her teeth into his neck with a sickening CRUNCH.

The sound was horrifying—a mixture of tearing flesh, the snap of cartilage, and the wet squelch of blood spilling from the wound.

Mitch tried to scream, but the force of the bite cut off any sound. His hands instinctively flew up to the Hag's head, trying to push her away, but the strength in his limbs was rapidly fading as her grasp had choked away his ability to breathe.

The Hag held on with the tenacity of a rabid dog, her jaws clamped down on Mitch's throat, gripping muscle and sinew with unholy strength. Then as quickly as she clamped on, she let go. Mitch stumbled and tried to keep his balance. He reached for the phone in his lab coat and dialed 9-1-1 before his senses left him. "I need help," he squelched. Then he slumped to the floor, his body twitching violently. The coroner's eyes rolled back into his head, his limbs spasming uncontrollably before he went still, his body collapsing.

The Hag collapsed back onto the steel table. Her lips, still wet with Mitch's blood, curled into a grotesque smile as she let out a final exhale. Her body convulsed once more, and then, as if some unseen force had been extinguished, she lay completely still. The grotesque mask of the Hag began to fade, her twisted features softening and receding, until the lifeless face of Vito Matthews stared back up at the cold, fluorescent lights.

Mitch's body lay on the cold unforgiving floor. The overhead lights continued to buzz and then, Mitch's body began to twitch and convulse, his limbs jerking in unnatural spasms. His eyes, suddenly rolled back into place, and were now filled with a wicked, hostile gleam. His mouth twitched, curling into a grotesque imitation of a smile as a low, raspy growl emanated from deep within his throat.

"Mary, Mary... quite contrary..." Mitch whispered, his voice oily with perverse pleasure, the words slithering out like poison.

Bloody Mary

The legend of **Bloody Mary** is a well-known urban myth, often associated with a ghostly figure said to appear in mirrors when her name is called repeatedly, usually three times. The myth has taken on various forms, but common threads include a vengeful spirit, death, and the supernatural. There are several interpretations of who Bloody Mary might be, each linked to real-life historical figures or folklore:

1. **Mary I of England (1516–1558)**: Mary Tudor, daughter of Henry VIII, is the most common historical figure associated with the Bloody Mary legend. She was known as "**Bloody Mary**" due to her persecution of Protestants during her reign, which led to the burning of many at the stake. Her attempts to restore Catholicism to England earned her a fearsome reputation. Some believe that the Bloody Mary legend reflects her spirit's unrest or anger over her troubled reign and tragic personal life (including her multiple false pregnancies).

2. **Other Interpretations**: Some versions of the legend suggest that Bloody Mary was a woman who died under tragic circumstances, such as being wronged or seeking vengeance. In this version, she appears when summoned through rituals, often tied to mirrors, candles, and dark settings, to exact revenge or communicate with the living.

3. **The Ritual**: According to the myth, if someone stands in front of a mirror in a darkened room and calls out "Bloody Mary" three times (or in some versions, more), her spirit will appear, sometimes to reveal the future or to cause harm. This mirrors the historical fascination

with divination and mirrors, which were often considered portals to the supernatural.

"Mary, Mary, Quite Contrary"

Mary, Mary, quite contrary,
How does your garden grow?
With silver bells and cockle shells,
And pretty maids all in a row.

The nursery rhyme **"Mary, Mary, Quite Contrary"** is often associated with a historical figure, much like Bloody Mary. There are different interpretations of the rhyme, each linking it to significant events and characters in history:

1. **Mary I of England (Bloody Mary)**: Some believe that the nursery rhyme refers to Mary I. The phrase "quite contrary" is thought to describe her difficult and controversial reign. The following lines of the rhyme are often interpreted as symbolic references:

   - **"How does your garden grow?"**: This could be a metaphor for her failed attempts to bear children or possibly refer to her reign's brutality, with "garden" symbolizing England and its troubled state under her rule.

   - **"With silver bells and cockle shells"**: Some interpretations suggest that these lines reference Catholicism, as "silver bells" could be the sanctus bells used in Catholic rituals, and "cockle shells" might refer to badges worn by pilgrims.
   - **"And pretty maids all in a row"**: This could refer to the execution of Protestant martyrs or the nuns and religious figures reinstated during her reign.

2. **Alternate Interpretations**:

- Some suggest the rhyme refers to **Mary, Queen of Scots**, another prominent Mary of the time. Her life was marked by political intrigue, betrayal, and imprisonment, which may have inspired parts of the rhyme. The "garden" in this context might symbolize her constant schemes and the upheaval in Scotland.

- Another theory ties the rhyme to a **Catholic allegory**. England's religious turmoil during Mary I's reign, especially her efforts to return the country to Catholicism, are thought to influence the symbolism in the rhyme.

I have endeavored to honor the lore as faithfully as possible while crafting a fully realized antagonist whose influence stretches across centuries. One thing is certain: the Hag will return with a vengeance.

Made in the USA
Columbia, SC
29 September 2024